THE TURQUOISE
WAR

For Mr. John Hunter,
I hope you enjoy my book! :)

To Mr John Hunter,
Shope Row,
orton
book.

THE TURQUOISE WAR

A. E. VARDAKIS

Copyright © 2014 by A. E. Vardakis.

Library of Congress Control Number: 2014907715
ISBN: Hardcover   978-1-4990-0144-0
              Softcover   978-1-4990-0145-7
              eBook   978-1-4990-0146-4

All rights reserved. No part of this book may be reproduced or transmitted in any form or by any means, electronic or mechanical, including photocopying, recording, or by any information storage and retrieval system, without permission in writing from the copyright owner.

This is a work of fiction. Names, characters, places and incidents either are the product of the author's imagination or are used fictitiously, and any resemblance to any actual persons, living or dead, events, or locales is entirely coincidental.

Any people depicted in stock imagery provided by Thinkstock are models, and such images are being used for illustrative purposes only.
Certain stock imagery © Thinkstock.

Rev. date: 04/25/2014

To order additional copies of this book, contact:
Xlibris LLC
1-800-455-039
www.xlibris.com.au
Orders@xlibris.com.au
521928

"This book is captivating and unpredictable, deep and insightful. It is a heart-warming story of morals, love, action, justice and intrigue that keeps you guessing until the end and hanging for more."

—*Deane K.*
Teacher

"A very captivating read that is flowing with imagination, drama, suspense and action. A great book for teenagers and young adults, which suspends disbelief and throws your mind into the future and a world beyond existence."
"Exciting and emotional read."

—*Peter Katsoulas*
Physiotherapist

"Everyone has an idea for a novel. Few people are actually brave enough to write it down. Stay brave and keep on writing!"

—*Mr. Boland*
Secondary Teacher

"Awesome science fiction for all ages. Riveting story telling."

—*A and S. Koutsoumbis*
Optometrist

"A great novel by a young and gifted writer. Easy to read, fast moving action, exciting plot, not a single dull page. Highly recommended especially to teen readers but can be enjoyed by all ages."

—*C. Jays*
Lawyer

"The Turquoise War was a blast to read, showcasing the talent of this young author. I couldn't take my eyes of the book, as the ingenious plot developed with every turning page. Surely an author to look out for in the future."

—*Cheran*
Year 9 student from Knox Grammar School

"Has been very interesting to read, well written and enjoyed reading it"

—*Sylvia*
Qantas Credit Union Banker

"I have to say, bravo. The whole plot of the story is well written having the characters unfolding and defined in their attempt to secure defense against a supposedly hostile alien race and vice versa against the human race. My favourite character in the book is Rasirine."

—*Paul Salakas*
Bank Manager CBA Mascot

"What a marvelous book with an intriguing adventure. I look forward to reading more of this talented young writer's work in the future."

—*Anne-Marie*
Secretary

"Fascinating and interesting story of what the future may hold! Very deep and meaningful story, kept me intrigued and wanting to read more. Well written shows we are all different but the same."

—*Liz B*
Customer Service Officer
Department of Human Services

"Having a young writer who is so dedicated and meticulous with detail is refreshing. The world she has created in her mind is truly unique in every way. She is clear and succinct at portraying her world to the reader and the raw emotion that is felt is none like I have ever experienced. I commend Athanasia on her first of what I believe will be many works, and I look forward to reading more in the years to come."

—*Tess*
Dentist

This book is dedicated to my mother, who supported me throughout the writing of this book and continues to support me. I would like also to dedicate this book to my English teacher Mr. Boland. Without his encouragement and help, I would have never committed myself to writing this book.

A special thank-you goes to both of them.

CHAPTER 1

London, Earth, 2572

Throughout my challenging life, I had a dreadful recurring dream troubling me night after night. It was immensely uncanny and frightening, but something was not letting me wake up from it.

In my dream a tall, beautiful woman was appearing constantly with a turquoise skin and golden hair dropping over her shoulders like the sun's rays. Her hair had this unique shine and sparkle resembling the stars in the dark sky. I do not remember this woman stating her name at any stage in my dreams.

The only words I remember her uttering were 'fire, pain, and death is near!' There was also a strange warning of a day coming in the near future that would turn 'Orchadia' into ashes. She said 'Orchadia' would burn, but the golden key would save it, and she would recite to me the same poem every night. She urged me to memorise it, and said that it was of great importance that I knew it well.

> The universe shall crash and burn,
> No one will try to fight,
> Or see their turn,

Go on straight through the long and endless night,
The secrets of Orchadia,
Are the ones we should hold dear,
For one will save Orchadia,
When the time is near,
The secrets shall protect us,
And end the war we fear,
The universe shall bow down,
It shall cry a tear,
No one will ever cast a frown,
Upon our great achievements that we've accomplished here'

'David, open your eyes! Are you all right?'

I opened my eyes slowly, allowing them to readjust to the new temperatures and light. Then I saw Rasirine. She smiled, and I was mesmerised by her blue hair glistening in the faded sunlight. And in her delicate tone of voice, she said, 'They have gone, we are safe for now.'

As I regained consciousness, I noticed the state of the city around me. Homes were reduced to ashes, buildings, mega complexes buried in dust and rocks, stray fires here and there, and dead bodies lying everywhere, blank eyes staring into nothing with the last face of fear sketched on their faces as they died defending what they believed in.

I saw that my clothes were torn and drenched in blood, my own blood that I meant to spill, blood of men and women just like me who died today under my knowledge, and under my power.

Whether they were bad or good, Neekans or humans, I shot them. I killed them. One beam of my laser gun sufficed to take their last breath. It was so easy but so dreadful at the same time. The feelings of pain and guilt rose up inside me, but I knew that I did not have a choice. It was either them or us. I was here to fight. To fight for the Neekans and to promote peace within the two races I so dearly love and care for. Ironic, is it not?

I was only nineteen when the war started, but somehow I do not remember anything good before that either. All my life has been misty and uncertain. All I know now was that here I am with Rasirine in this torn-up tent, starving for food with the sole purpose to kill every living thing that possessed danger and threat to us. *Us* meaning the ones without the 'mark'.

Rasirine, as she was bandaging my bleeding wounds, uttered in an anxious and disappointing voice, 'This is wrong. We should not kill them, David. They have a life too!'

Through my excruciating pain, I was able to nod humbly, but Rasirine wanted to make sure that I understood, and she said, 'They have hurt your people, they have betrayed my people, but you know what the right thing to do is? We should not have to kill them.'

Seeing how the pain in her eyes was escalating by them becoming teary at every word she was pronouncing, it hurt me even more than words could describe. She certainly did not want this enmity to continue. She did not want her people or my people to die under any circumstances. However, deep down, Rasirine knew very well that this was not our choice.

The human race is special apparently!? The human race is a race of great prosperity and intellect. Humans are a race that has defied so many other species of creatures, as everyone has told me, and everyone is convinced of this fact. This is what I have learnt at school and at college.

During tutorials, I was exposed to the same repetitive information of little or no substance, day after day after day. I heard stories about how 'we' humans being the most superior creatures. I have heard also about how the Neekans, on coming here, brought prosperity that was unimaginable. Prosperity that all other life in the colossal universe was envious of, but we humans were still better than them.

On the other hand, the Neekans were described as being satanic and demonic creatures who should be tortured and left to rot on the roads for all to see, that they were nothing more but a concoction of the devil that was here to send us all to hell. I heard so many other stories, fabricated out of ignorance and created out of idiocy in order to satisfy the stupid human need of feeling superior when in reality, we are nothing great at all!

For humans to use power to hurt and enslave definitely is not power at all, but it can rather be described as weakness. A weakness developed only in the thick and dim-witted brains of the ones who think that they represent the higher classes of society. The ones who wish to assume great power and influence over others.

Thoughts enslave many of the restricting beliefs within us, but there are the few that leave this slavery and find themselves thinking in a way much different than their own kind. Unfortunately, for those who stay horribly positioned in their closed mindset of evil and nastiness interpret everything that is new and different in an odious way.

Those who are engulfed by acceptance for others and have love in their heart would not be under the 'dull' impression that the things they have not met before are evil and satanic. However, they would not allocate any judgment based on what rumors they have heard before. They would try to perceive how much kindness those creatures possess. Yet I am the only one who saw these enchanting creatures in this light. I can vouch with certainty that no one would ever befriend them and care for them.

My 'supposedly special' species enslaved those other creatures. We tortured them and took all their gifts and treasures. We used anything we could against them, and in order to hurt them, we did this with the murder of their children so that we instill fear and force them into peaceful service. Yes, we did all these savage things and yet we dare to label ourselves as 'such a special race'.

I am just a human, just an average human with average intelligence, from a decent family but nothing special. My mother says I am very unique and important, but looking at the whole picture, I am one of twelve billion humans on the planet Earth. I am 'nothing' but a minuscule part of this world in comparison to the vast and unimaginably colossal universe. I am as inconspicuous as a grain of sand and as tiny as an atom that cannot be seen with a naked eye.

I am like millions of other children born in this wonderful city of London in the year of the Emperor Kosler 2548. Many hundred years ago, it was said that the city was flourishing like never before. It was called the most advanced city of the world! It is hard to imagine its then beauty now. In many scripts, it was described as having clean blue skies free of all pollutants, mega complexes embellished with golden swirl works of art towering high above the roads with an advanced technology elegantly designing and assisting almost every possible human need by putting forward with extraordinary ability, fantastic buildings of all different shapes and sizes crafted with the finest glass off the moons of Belfoyr.

In those times existed the finest restaurants, the most radiant clothing and fashion embellished with charm and distinguished originality. It was the first city to be visited by the alien race of the Neekans.

At first, everyone was so frightened of them, but soon enough, our government formed a partnership of harmony with the Neekans. I suspect that this was mainly the result of this fear of being under the Neekans' rule and dominance. I do not see why though; they were such a magical race, so much more than we could ever be, so kind and gentle, so ever respectful of our cultures and our children, and so beautiful in every respect. Just as always, my people did not understand them. No one did, and it seemed that no one wanted to either.

The message was clear—we were to live in peace with the visitors, but to never make it more than cohabiting with them. For those who wished to go beyond the understanding of just living in 'peace' with the Neekans and form friendships the Neekans, there was a strict and non-negotiable punishment. Those who befriended the Neekans were to be sent to the underground facility which was a horrid world of dirt, betrayal and filth. A world of slavery and arduous pain and sufferance where disease set in and would rot and wither the body in agonizing pain as they were living their short and final days.

However, the city of London no longer portrays the magnificent world as it was once before. It is just darkness, a tiny concealed hell where no one is accepted in our area unless they have the 'mark'.

Our government was ripped apart by our own foolish ignorance. The prevailing ignorance threatened also the peaceful living society by shaking the strong foundations of 'peace' established many hundreds of years ago. It was ruined by stubborn, power-hungry people. Almost everyone is dead now, Neekans and humans, with the exception of a few left behind on Earth, including Rasirine and I.

CHAPTER 2

London, Year 2565

Anarchy broke out in all the countries around the world as the Neekans attacked and attempted to destroy the governments. They first attacked and killed the presidents of the countries; all the officials are dead. People are taken from their homes every day. Wherever the Neekans are, they are coming for 'us' humans.

'Look at the headline', I called out to my mother, who was totally uninterested in anything that was related to the Neekans. The Neekans were rising against our laws and killing our people. Probably they wanted to create chaos before order settled in on our planet Earth. My mother preferred to stay in her own little world. She was not even aware of the great destruction taking place all around her. I was not sure if my mother was dealing with this whole upheaval by employing a purposeful mechanism to dwell in oblivious bliss.

I continued reading the article silently, my eyes scanning every little detail of information coming through each black-and-white word formed on the lexicogram. In futile desperation, I was looking for a piece of information that was going to induce some feelings of hope and ignite the desire to keep on going no matter what. Instead, an overwhelming feeling of fear dominated the essence of my thoughts. However, I kept reading on anyway.

My mother asked me, 'What is so important about that article David? You have glued your whole face in the printed word?'

I responded with hesitation, 'Glaron is enslaved in Chicago. I spoke to him yesterday on contactogram. He is being so badly treated by our people, but he said that he will tolerate whatever comes his way. He didn't want to disclose anything about the attacks. Do you think he is safe?'

There was no response from my mother.

'Mum! Are you even listening to me!?'

Then she responded in a startling tone of voice, as if she was waking up from a dream. 'What, David? Oh! Yes, Glaron, lovely 'thing'. Too bad he is not a human. You two could have been the best of friends.'

My mother, just like every other human being on this planet, lived in ignorance of the fact that these were creatures of peace and love, yet we caged them and had them as our slaves. Not anymore though. Now we were starting a revolution. Hand in hand, I, Rasirine, and Glaron and all our other Neekan and human supporters would rise up against the constant misery we were being put through. Mother, though she would never speak of it, knew what we were up to, and so she would not let me see my friends, for she was dreading the time the officials would take me to the underground.

I could tell that part of her resented the fact that she had not produced a normal child. When she was called to the school and told that 'David, her son', in the hover ground, was found every day, playing with the Neekan children (and that my best friend Rasirine was one of them), I was grounded and forbidden attendance to my school.

'Mum, does it really matter if he is a Neekan? He has rights too! Besides, now with the new cellular discoveries, it is proven that they possess similar genomes to us. Except that they are nicer.' My mother shot me a glare and looked at the cameras that were surveying the city.

I rolled my eyes. 'A human and a Neekan will be allowed to marry. I will help lead our new generation into accepting and allowing interspecies marriage, when that law will pass of course.'

'Do not start again with that law! They are alien!' Her face was gaining colour, and I knew this was not something she wanted to discuss.

I saw her point of view, but that did not mean that I had agreed. She was afraid of the Neekans, and that was because everyone was taught to be afraid of them.

I responded with an air of frustration to my mother. 'You do know that my best friends are Neekans. They are just as human as us, Mum, but with a slight difference that they are much kinder than us and they show respect for us.'

'How do they respect us, David?' Mother replied, and I did not know if I had to answer, but I did.

'They have shown respect towards us because they have helped us immensely! Why will you not appreciate them for who they are?'

My mother lowered her voice and whispered softly, 'Do not let the guards of the city hear you say that! They will remove you and send you to the underground services, and I cannot afford losing you, David!'

I realised that this argument of trying to convince my mother otherwise was of no use. I knew that deep down in my heart, I was right. So what if I was to be taken to the underground? The Neekans deserved respect just as much as we do. This made me even more determined to find a way to put this into perspective.

I tried calling Glaron again on my contactogram. No response. I sent him a message to his portal pod and waited for a reply. I waited three hours and twenty-three minutes. Still nothing! At this point, most people in my situation would have panicked, but I didn't. I trusted his instinct. But another thought stirred in my head, which enslaved me even further as I was waiting for Glaron's call. 'Why was there need for the Neekans to attack?' I was trying in vain to look for a decent explanation.

CHAPTER 3

'Rasirine, you will be killed. We should not be here together!' Rasirine's smile warmed my heart. As we sat here underneath the tangerine sky watching the sun set into the beach, I knew Rasirine was going to be punished, and I knew it was going to be my fault.

I held her hand, and a tear slid down her face as I whispered to her that we would definitely stop this slavery from continuing. So what if she was not a human? So what if this was forbidden? Rasirine was the kindest creature on this earth, and I wanted to help her regain her rights.

Rasirine was our servant. My mother's servant to be clear, but from the moment I saw her, I felt through her calmness that there was great pain and misery governing her soul. Day after day, Rasirine was always happy to attend to my needs; she would help me with my homework and cheer me up in my not-so-good days. And more likely in my unhappy days, she would be there for me and put a smile on my face. I grew up having Rasirine's presence in our large home, but I never saw where she was going when she was not in our home. I was under the impression that she would have occupied the guest room during this time since she was spending all of her time with us.

I recall constantly asking my mother where Rasirine went to sleep at night and what was she having for food. My mother would immediately ask me to go to my room and denied me an answer to my questions. I could not understand why Rasirine and I were different. I did not like the fact that she was in our home only to be given orders to and for her to follow them.

'Mum, Rasirine is such a nice girl. Why can she not be my friend?'

My mother replied with a stern look, 'Because you are too naïve to understand!'

'And why does she have scars?' I insisted this time to get an answer. My mother looked at me and felt the desperation in my eyes to get a response, so she promised to explain to me some other time because it was quite an elaborated answer that she had to provide to me with. She didn't miss the chance to remind me that she had asked me to go my room.

'Oh, and why can she not eat her meals with us at the holotable?' I quickly managed to ask her my third question, to which I knew I wasn't going to get an answer. But anyway, I tried.

My mother, whose emotions I could read ever so easily, was in great difficulty at answering any of the questions I asked about Rasirine. She would only say, 'She is our slave. She is an alien. She cannot be given rights because she will take advantage of us. She is not as a "good" person as she appears to be, and I forbid you to speak to her!' Her voice vibrating like a thunderbolt grew a fear of her inside of me. 'Never speak of that vermin again! Is that understood?'

I was so afraid that I did not think twice about leaving the lounge room and quickly ran to my room. I shut the door behind me and made a few steps towards my bed and sat on it. After some pondering, tears came down from my eyes. I ended up crying for hours. I was not even in the mood to watch the portal-pod, I did not eat for days, and I even threatened to leave home if I was not going to get any answers to my questions in each and every visit that my mother paid to my room. However, my mother seemed to know that I was not really meaning to carry out my threats and that it was a temporary reaction. She knew that I was bluffing, so she never took seriously whatever empty threats I was throwing at her, no matter how outrageous or ridiculous they may have sounded.

Going back, on my tenth birthday, I told my mother that I had made my choice. I made her aware that I was going to get the Neekans' "mark". I was going to fight and support the Neekans even if that decision meant to sacrifice my life. My determination to carry out what I really wanted to do had never failed me before, and this time, my decision was final.

CHAPTER 4

With every day passing, I was growing up with Rasirine. She was my closest friend, my sister, my companion, my confidant. I felt Glaron, Rasirine, and I were like the three musketeers from centuries ago.

Rasirine is a very caring soul. In her available time, she was teaching me some new Neekan games that were second nature to her since she had mastered them whilst she was with her people. Learning how to play the new Neekan games was my favourite pastime. Each time I was under the impression that I had mastered a new Neekan game, I could not wait to compete with Rasirine in order to prove my competence. Through these games, Rasirine would not only teach me about the rules, but she would also educate me about the history of the games. The information that she was sharing with me was opening a door about her world, the Neekans' habits, nature, and supreme knowledge.

I grew to feel a strong liking and admiration for the Neekans through Rasirine's sharpened mind. I was impressed by the details of knowledge she had on many historical events about us, humans.

Rasirine asked whilst teaching me one of the games in the hope that I would be able to confirm her information, 'David, did you know that in 2013, NASA, a humans' scientific research team for the universe, was able to cultivate vegetable patches on the moon?'

I was taken by surprise and responded, 'No, I was not aware of this historical detail. We humans tried to view the moon as an alternative place to live in case Earth was to be destroyed.' I wanted to find out more about the Neekans' knowledge and intentions and said to Rasirine, 'It seems contradictory for a "peaceful" race like the Neekans resulting in violence and creating chaos on planet Earth when their intention was to bring peace. How can this be achieved if there is so much killing taking place?'

Rasirine took a deep breath. 'There is a logical explanation for it. The Neekans wish to wipe out "all evil" from planet Earth, and in achieving this, they thought it would be best to start from your leaders, the presidents and officials as you call them.'

'Rasirine I promise you that I am going to do whatever it takes to end this slavery of the Neekans by humans once and for all.'

I was so excited with her stories especially when she would tell me about all the astounding different colours that existed in the universe and about their amazing spaceships, which were decorated with thousands of different-shaped buttons, gadgets, and gizmos.

We spoke and played for hours on end especially when my mother was sleeping after her long tiring days of work in the galaxy.

Rasirine attended my school too, and that was a blessing in itself, for we could share a lot of time together with another two Neekans after classes. The Great Emperor Jarodas College was one of the worst schools that ever existed. It was separating the Neekans as being a lower class than the humans. But Rasirine seemed to enjoy frequenting it. Little did she know that humans didn't think much of the Neekans. She liked almost everything about The Great Emperor Jarodas College. The only thing she did not like was that she wasn't in the same sector as me. She was in the Neekan's sector where all the other Neekan children were allocated to be.

The Neekan children were allowed to attend The Great Emperor Jarodas College under the condition that they were kept at a safe distance away from human children. My science teacher was pretty adamant about us human children keeping away from the Neekan children.

Human children were glad and ecstatic about attending The Great Emperor Jarodas College, but for me, school was torture as my best friends were Neekans. I could not disclose this aspect of my secret life to anyone. I was constantly enslaved in a thinking process of trying to find a solution on how to bring the two races together. My thinking process was dominated by these thoughts permanently.

It was enormously exasperating and irritating not being able to share my views openly with my fellow humans. How was 'globalisation' realised some hundreds of years ago amongst humans? There was very little information in order for me to get some ideas. Why could not cohabitation with the Neekans be achieved in peace and as easily as the globalisation process?

I had developed this belief for the past few years that I should not be considering myself being as a human any more since I was tended to be appreciated more and more by the Neekan children whom I considered them to be my only real friends in comparison to any other human children that I had met.

I recall waiting by the side gate of the school precisely at 4.08 p.m. to meet up with my Neekan friends, and by 4.09 p.m. if they were not there, I would get all anxious and absolutely desperate by 4:10 p.m. I was enjoying immensely the time spent together with my Neekan friends especially when we would go and buy cosmic-gelatos. I always savored the purchase of a triple-chocolate-flavoured cosmic-gelato.

Rasirine liked the lemon taste, and Glaron was fond of the reddish colours, so he preferred the strawberry-flavoured cosmic-gelato. We would always make fun of him for choosing the strawberry-flavoured cosmic-gelato because even in the Neekans' culture, the strawberry-flavoured cosmic-gelatos were more favoured by their girls. Kirlan, another Neekan friend of mine, indulged in the orange sherbet taste.

Being around my Neekan friends was such a joy. I recall the hours spent playing at the local hover park. I greatly enjoyed the games even though I was appearing to be a little bit awkward in them.

Glaron said that I resembled a newborn deer trying to take its first steps into a new world. Given the then-current situation in time, it was not a very good analogy to be compared to a deer because those animals had become extinct in 2490. It was something that exceedingly saddened me.

I was trying very hard to get accustomed to the Neekans' world. I was not allowed to spend much time with them, and this was making things difficult for me. One bright solution that both my Neekan friends and I adopted was to create our own cryptic language.

My Neekan friends and I had developed this covert language in order to be able to communicate easier without being understood, and we organised our secret meetings and gatherings. Human rules wanted Neekan children away from human children. But we found a way to defy the rules.

We constantly kept refining our secret language and adding more sounds to represent different meanings through mental holograms containing various arrays of seemingly unconnected secret images, decoding messages for a specific meeting at a precise time in the cybermall, virtual beach, or park.

I grew so close to my friends to the point where I considered them to be my extended family. It didn't really matter that we were different. Emotionally, we were the same.

My mother was married to a high official, my father, who did not care about me at all. He had left me all alone in the house many times crying, feeling unwanted and hurt. My only escape and solace was when I was inviting my Neekan friends over. I tried to do this as often as I could. I loved it when we were discussing and debating over whether or not our school canteen should start serving cooked fly-fish rather than the constant raw and particularly unhygienic green ones.

It was an interesting aspect of conversations then because I was able to learn and understand better my Neekan friends. We were exchanging fruitful ideas of how to make small changes, and if they were successful, then we were to proceed to make bigger changes in our universe.

When we were getting tired from the in-depth discussions, we would play twistobots and watch the latest teen dramas. This was not to say that our friendship did not have the ups and downs of any 'normal' friendship. We also had our moments of strong disagreements and petty arguments and silly competitions. I remember we had this 'stupid' competition of how to best attract Rasirine's attention. Rasirine, of course, did not know anything about it. We all liked Rasirine, and we all tried to compete against one another so we could get Rasirine's attention. But Rasirine shyly admitted that it was me that she was fond of.

I was the happiest boy in the whole universe when Rasirine timidly and so sweetly confessed that she preferred me over the other boys. From that day on, Rasirine and I grew even closer together.

I asked Rasirine, 'Please, Rasirine, let's promise to never keep any secrets or hide any information from each other'.

'Yes, David, I promise! I promise for honesty to prevail in our friendship at all times.'

Probably, this was not a very good idea because I recall the time when Rasirine, in order to keep her promise, disclosed that there was a time where she fancied Glaron. I felt a little uncomfortable. I did not know what to say because my ego was under attack.

When Rasirine saw this uncomfortable feeling taking over me, she said, 'Let's not talk again about our past and even our future feelings of affection and attraction that we may have for another human or Neekan'.

I just nodded my head in affirmative.

On my thirteenth birthday, when my mother was out to buy some sunlight cake, I told Rasirine, 'You are very important to me, Rasirine, and I want us to be together forever'.

Rasirine smiled and softly replied, 'Forever is a very long time, David. The future has a strange way of changing many things'. And a tear rolled down her velvet turquoise cheeks.

I hated seeing Rasirine feeling sad. 'Please, Rasirine, do not be sad. Do you know that every time you smile, my insides churn? And do you know that with just one smile of yours, you make me feel very happy for hours during the whole day?'

She slowly lifted her head and smiled at me again.

As I sat there looking at her in the eyes, I explained to her what I thought about the Neekans. I told her about how much respect I had for her and her people, but I could not help it to ask questions others would not dare to ask.

'Rasirine, I mean not to be rude, but why are your people here?'

'David, I come from a galaxy far, far away, from the Crystalone Galaxy, ten billion lightyears away. My planet is called Orchadia, a prosperous beautiful planet with skies of orange lit by four suns by sending their warm rays to our planet.'

'What about at nighttime? Do you have nighttime in Orchadia?'

'In Orchadia, yes, of course we also have nighttime. Our planet has six moons that keep the blue trees alive and strong for centuries. My planet has also mountains so high that sparkle golden from lightyears away. We also have kingdoms, and I am the princess of Orchadia. But my planet, for the last ten lightyears, is suffering. This is the reason why we came to planet Earth.'

'I do not understand, Rasirine. What are you trying to tell me?'

'We are here to get your help, David. This is why we killed the leaders because we do not have time to go through negotiations, and it is the only way for you humans to follow us without having to listen to your leaders and officials. We tried to leave you with only one choice—to listen and follow the Neekans' instructions—but our plan has dreadfully failed. David, you are the key to the salvation of Orchadia.'

'You are . . . you are a princess!' I looked at her with awe.

According to Rasirine's description, her planet, her world, seemed so wonderful, so magical showered in skies of orange sprinkled with rays from four suns. It sounded like a wonderful world of serenity, so different from our own world. It was so fascinating. However, the name Orchadia seemed to ring a bell, but I could not pinpoint where I had heard it before. I could not believe what I was hearing. I was a simple boy who had become best friends with an angel from the stars, and my destiny was to be the salvation of a planet? It was all too much for me.

'But, Rasirine, I am just a boy. What could I possibly do to help your race?'

'David, do not tell me that you do not know that you have already been helping us?'

'How? I only have some thoughts on how to help you escape from slavery. Perhaps, the Neekans can rebel against the humans and start a revolution with the aim of creating an equal society for both humans and Neekans.'

'We have already started the revolution by killing the leaders'

'Rasirine, you know how much I care for you and your people, the Neekans, but I also care for my own people because we are not all bad.

I am sure that in your race you also have the "bad apples", as we say in human language. I will stand by you and give you all the strength you need and hope to save your planet Orchadia.'

'I have faith in you, David. I know what I am asking you to do is extremely frightening, but before leaving Orchadia in search for help in the other galaxies, I was told a prophecy that a boy named David is the key to the salvation of Orchadia. This boy is in planet Earth of the Milky Way galaxy.'

'How do your people know about me?'

'David, trust me, you are the only human who can help us for you may be young but you see with the eyes of the holy and the affectionate. There is one man creating all this pain to both humans and Neekans. Humans are not all at fault.'

'Rasirine, this is all too confusing for me!'

'Listen carefully to what I am going to tell you—'

'Shhh! I think somebody is coming!'

'It is Glaron, keeping an eye at the entrance of the door.'

'OK! I am listening, Rasirine.'

'We Neekans are much afraid of you humans. As we are such a prosperous race, we want not to be your slaves. Many of us have already retaliated and armed ourselves against you, but our elders in my race advised us to work in a partnership with human if we want their cooperation.'

'Then why did you burn and kill most humans?'

'We never thought that we would ever meet a human that we would be able to admire. I have seen your innocence, David, and I am touched by your honesty, bravery, and kindness.'

How could I have not seen this? On both sides of a game, there is always the one who wins and the one that loses. But it is also true that we can have both sides win.

Humans and Neekans need not to fight, neither enslave, one another. However, most people close their minds to equality and peace and see no option but to fight and conquer in order to declare themselves as winners.

Life is treated like a game for the grown-ups. They do not distinguish the difference between the virtual games of pretending to take life away and the real game played by the people who enjoy war and do not care when others die.

They do not see that they are actually slaying their own spirit. Our life, our decisions, our homes and families are all dependent on certain people's ideologies.

Humans have witnessed the harm caused by the fourteen billion years of Earth's existence, but we never seem to want to change our ways.

Rasirine extended her arm and touched me on my shoulder.

I immediately stopped my silent thinking. 'I promise you I will spread the word of peace and equality for your race. Tell me who is this man who is creating this pain to both our races, and I shall find him and remove him from his position.'

'You want to kill him, David? Is that what you aspire to do? You want to save our race by killing one of your men?'

'Why not, Rasirine!? If this is what it takes, I will do it. I love your people, and seeing you all being in this misery day after day hurts me! He isn't worth it! He isn't worth whatever money or fame or power that he receives!' I yelled.

A banging on the front door interrupted us. 'Don't tell her about the, plans all right? I promise you, I will help your people.'

For a moment, I thought it was my mother entering the house quickly, but it wasn't her. Three city guards broke down the door, bolted from the inside, with laser guns and pointed them straight at me and Rasirine, and particularly yelled at Rasirine.

'Hands up, all! The cameras of the city watch each and every one of you.' There was a short pause, which made his voice sound even louder and frightening.

'Where are your mother and your father, boy?' Before I could utter a decent answer, the guard roared to Rasirine. 'And you, sick thing, go back to your basement!'

His leather clothing covered his body, and thick black sunglasses shaded his eyes from our view. For a moment, I thought I saw a shine of blue, but perhaps it was just a trick of the light. The guards came towards us and took hold of Rasirine and me. I was not going to let them take us without a fight. I struggled to free myself, but to no avail.

The guard was holding me down and could not focus his attention on Rasirine too because he had to make sure that I was kept captive.

One of the other two guards yelled at Rasirine, 'Who will you chose, you freak? The boy or yourself!? Or perhaps both of you can kneel down before us and beg for forgiveness?'

I could hardly project my voice after the struggle with the guard, but I managed to ask, 'Beg for forgiveness? Why? We have not done anything wrong!'

'We know what you are up to! Human-Neekan war plans and relationships . . . how you dare insult our race, you alien!' the guard shouted.

'No, please! Leave him! Take me to the underground, but do not hurt the boy. Do not hurt the boy!' Tears flooded Rasirine's face.

'Get upm you filth', the guard frothed and made Rasirine stand against the wall so the second guard could take aim at Rasirine's heart.

'Face your death with dignity, Rasirine!' I yelled out to her.

Rasirine stood up, held her head high, but could not contain some tears rolling down her face. The tears had a special kind of shine as they were rolling down her turquoise cheeks. She appeared to be ever so beautiful with the tiny stars glittering on her face.

Then she turned to face me without wiping the tears from her face but managed to utter in her sweet voice, 'I fear not the pain of death but the pain I will cause you because of my death, David. You have treated my people kindly. You are the golden key. You must fight and save the universe'.

The guard stood, laughing maniacally, and then he shot.

Nothing happened.

He checked his gun and shot again. But nothing happened for the second time. The guard swung around and looked questioningly at the other two guards.

I swiftly released myself from the guard after kicking him unexpectedly and called out, 'Never underestimate the speed, bravery, and intelligence of youth, sir!'

The guards turned around and, in bewilderment, saw in my hands two guns and the laser from the gun that the guard was trying to shoot Rasirine with.

'How did you get those, boy!?' the guard yelled.

One of them tried to storm towards me but held back when he saw that I was ready to fire. Suddenly alarmed at the loss of their weapons, the other guard reached for the intercom.

With an air of satisfaction, I asked the guard, 'Really? Did you think I would take your guns and leave your intercom working? Please, gentlemen, do not insult my intelligence'.

Rasirine got up and slowly walked away from the guards. When she was at a safe distance away from them, she came and stood next to me. The guards tried to run towards us to get the guns and to stop us from firing at them, but it was too late.

I gave Rasirine one of the guns and asked her in a voice that was full of confidence I had never felt before, 'Ready to fight, Ras?'

'You bet, David! But please no guns! No more killing!'

We stormed towards the guard after throwing down the guns and fought them with our bare hands. I kicked one of the guards in the shin and elbowed the other in the eye. Rasirine knocked the third guard out with a glass vase that shattered at the impact, leaving him unconscious. The other two guards insisted on fighting on.

Rasirine, with the distinguished elegance of the turquoise-skinned people, swirled the guard on the floor, and I took on the other guard. I was so excited to acquaint his face with my fists. Probably it was not the smoothest and happiest meeting, but it had to be done. Then I gave him a gushing nose. He stood up again and picked up the table as a weapon. From the corner of my eye, I saw Rasirine bleeding heavily from a cavity in her arm as she pulled out the pocketknife lodged in her arm.

Both guards were regaining strength; after all, we were only two children fighting experienced soldiers. I scanned the living room; it was a complete mess. Parts of the broken door lay on the ground, and our papers and items were thrown everywhere. The chairs and table were lying in shreds, and the two guards were coming towards us like bloodthirsty monsters.

Whilst I was looking around for an escape, I heard this unfamiliar voice coming from the back of the room. 'I am Sir Sofron. I am in charge of these men. We will meet again, David, but next time, I will win.'

Without turning back to see who Sir Sofron was in the face, I looked at Rasirine and quickly said to her, 'Rasirine! Through the window!'

'It's a big drop, David!' she called out. 'We cannot jump!'

Initially, I thought that she was going to refuse to follow me, but after smashing the window with a sudden kick, we both jumped through the broken glass, holding each other's hand, waiting for our imminent death below.

CHAPTER 5

For a split second, I closed my eyes, and it felt like we were falling for a long time. We cut through the air as we were falling, and the wind was rushing around us. I could feel the cold breeze beating against my skin and through my clothes, freezing me straight to the bone.

I opened my eyes to see where we were going to land. With relief, I saw that instead of landing on hard cold cement, there was a big area covered with large black rubbish bags lined on the ground. *We might survive this*, I thought. And then I blacked out.

'David . . . David where are we? Why does it stink here?' I heard Rasirine asking in a disorientated and confused voice.

'My head hurts. I think that I hurt my head. Are you all right?'

I regained consciousness and got up immediately, ready to attack if necessary. After noticing that everything was safe I turned to Rasirine to reassure her and said, 'Well, I actually do not know. Where do you think we are, Ras?'

'I do not know either!'

'Perhaps on the moon? Maybe we are on the moon! Is that not lovely?'

'Really? We are on the moon! We are good teleporting like that!'

'I know, right? It smells like a rubbish dump! A rubbish dump on the moon! It feels like a rubbish dump. Maybe we have fallen on the rubbish collector on the moon! Are we still alive?' I gave her a cheeky grin.

She giggled and punched me playfully in the arm. 'Yes, we are alive, and I am pretty sure we are not on the moon, but I am sure we are safe.'

My smile faded for a moment because I knew that we were not safe. Anywhere I was with Rasirine, she would always be in danger. 'Rasirine, this is my fault. We are safe only for now.'

'No, it is not! It is your fault just as much as it is mine, but why did you say only for now? Do you think the guards would still be after us?' Her voice was filled with concern, and as she tried to pick herself up to come closer to me, I noticed a deep burn on her leg, and she fell back onto the rubbish bags.

'Are you all right, Ras? Let me see your burn.'

'Oh, this? It is nothing, it will be fine. I can heal very easily.'

I watched Rasirine's turquoise skin glow into a soft emerald colour as she touched softly her wound with her other hand. Within a few seconds, another layer of turquoise skin formed over the burnt area. Her bleeding arm had also patched itself together. A few seconds later, she leaned back against me, gazing at the partially visible stars.

'How is it that you heal so rapidly, Ras? I was watching the healing process on your turquoise skin and it looked painless, fast, and peaceful.'

Rasirine tried to respond, but as I leaned forward, my head hurt, and the pain reminded me of my gash.

'It is easy, David, let me help you heal too.' She slightly touched my wound, and a shiver of delight fled down my spine. I did not know whether that was caused by the sensation of being healed, or it was just my excitement of Rasirine's presence being here with me.

Within moments, the pain from my wound was gone. I stared at her blue eyes, flickering so beautifully in the moonlight. I held her hand. She was so delicate and fragile and yet very strong in her own way. I never wanted her to be in danger again because of me.

Rasirine was so proud of me. 'That was amazing, David, you saved us! And may I say quite a clever move you made there. How did you block their intercom?'

The admiration Rasirine felt for me was making me feel like the happiest person on Earth. I never thought my computer engineering class at school would come in handy ever, but much to my disbelief, it did.

'I didn't save you, Ras. We're a good team, that's all.'

I drifted off, thinking how dull and monotonous my life would be if I had never met Rasirine. Glaron, on the other hand, was too great to handle. What upset me most was the fact that Rasirine was faced with danger because of me.

Uneasily, I restarted my sentence. 'Oh, that's nothing, just some simple reconstruction of the main wiring interface', I said, appearing so knowledgeable and intelligent.

Rasirine was feeling kind of lost, but she smiled nevertheless. I felt obliged to further explain precisely how it happened and continued, 'It was quite simple, Ras. Really, all I had to do was to remove the main remote and change the buttons'. She then giggled.

'I know what you did. I come from far, far away, remember? I just love it when you speak to me as if you are very clever. Every time that you explain things to me as if I am a child, I get happy butterflies in my stomach.'

I could not believe what I was hearing Rasirine saying. She said that she felt like she was a child. We had just gone through a broken glass window, five hundred levels above the ground, fought three mad guards, and sustained minor injuries, which Rasirine healed with her universal powers. She must be a pretty adventurous child.

'Butterflies have not been around for centuries, how could you know about them?'

There was something so magical and mystical about her knowledge of my home, Earth.

'What else do you know about humans, Ras?'

'Back in Orchadia, our main subject at school was about extraterrestrial creatures. We studied the Earth and also the planet of the Zidrads, which was not quite fun at all. We studied your behaviours and your values.'

'Do you mean about slavery and the way we carry on today with the Neekans?'

'No, no! Actually, one of your chief leaders on human "dignity", whom I have great respect for from your history, is Nelson Mandela. I think he died some four hundred years ago in your Earth time, precisely on 5 December 2013.'

'Of course, I remember him too from our history lessons. His aim was to free his people from slavery, and this is exactly what I am going to do, Rasirine, for your people, the Neekans.'

Rasirine looked at me with admiration and happily smiled. 'I always loved Earth the most from all the other planets. I always wanted to visit your Milky Way galaxy, and when the beholders of the truth said the time had come, I left for Earth to find the golden key: you, David!'

I was going to ask her what she meant by the golden key as she had said it twice before, but I looked above and saw the two guards looking in the darkness to find us.

'Don't look up, Ras. They're watching us', I whispered.

Rasirine moved silently some bags to the side which was wide enough for the two of us to fit in and quickly slid under them and covered her skin. She made a signal with her hand for me to go under, and I swerved in my stomach and hid with her.

We waited for them to go and hopefully give up their attempt to keep searching for us. As we waited for a few seconds, we heard feeble footsteps coming closer and closer. The unbearable stench from the rubbish was filling up our noses. It was quite uncomfortable, but we would not dare move.

We suddenly heard the guard's voice, calling out, 'Where is my daughter?'

The guard, evidently a weak man, was limping towards the rubbish. When he was two steps away from us, he stopped.

We heard him speak. 'I saw you both falling. It was I who guided you to run towards the window and to jump out of it so that you would fall on a safe landing.'

I did not understand what the guard was saying. Why was he asking for his daughter? Who was his daughter? Probably he meant Rasirine, but I had to find out.

'Rasirine, is not your child, sir! You are a human', I called out of the bags.

'And I will fight for her and protect her. It is my duty to keep her safe! Do not dare come anywhere near her!'

He removed his mask, and his skin glowed in a strong turquoise colour.

'Is this proof for you? I never meant to hurt Rasirine. I have not seen her for four hundred years. Let me see her.'

Rasirine's eyes filled with tears. 'Go, Ras! He is your dad. You will be safe with him.'

'No, David, he is not my father! You are imagining things.'

I could not understand what was happening because I was seeing Rasirine slowly retreating from the rubbish and walking over to her father. I heard him whisper something into her ear something along the lines of 'the one'. She embraced the guard, and they were both crying out of joy for seeing one another again after four centuries.

'Come, boy. Let me tell you of my intentions upon coming to your home.'

'What do you mean, sir?'

'I came not to injure or hurt anyone from your people, though I came with human company that did intend to do so.'

This did not make sense. Humans and Neekans were not on good terms. They had not been ever since the treaty was revoked.

'Sir, with all due respect, Rasirine and I could have been killed.'

'No matter, my boy, I would have healed both of you.'

Rasirine whispered something into her father's ear, and then she said loudly, 'Father, he is! But we must prepare him for it soon'. And then she looked over at me.

'Prepare me for what, Ras?' I asked.

'For the burning of Orchadia', she said.

I suddenly felt a strong kick on my left leg. I saw Rasirine trembling, frightfully curled up next to me. Was I imagining things now?

CHAPTER 6

Next thing I remember, I am in a spaceship far more amazing than imagination could ever conceive. They had kidnapped me. Rasirine and her dad had kidnapped me! I felt the hate of my fellow humans rise up in me, but then the wisdom of the elder Neekans I was taught growing up brought the anger down.

As I looked around, I saw that the doors were golden, and the control panels lit up with all the colours of the rainbow; the seats were glowing in a bright emerald green colour decorated with sparkles. Then there was this fresh smell emanating from the spaceship, resembling the scent of the wet earth. It was so natural and beautiful, just like home.

I noticed that I was lying on a comfortable warm bed with a platter of food beside me. Whether or not this was kidnapping, they had only peaceful means. This was not an evil act. They had brought me here for good.

'He has awaken', a soothing voice in the distance said.

I was well acquainted with this voice. It was Rasirine's voice. She approached me and sat next to me. As she was observing me, she tried to reassure me by saying, 'Do not worry! You are safe. I brought you to my home. The home I had missed for four hundred years.'

I did not understand what she was saying because I thought that she was only fifteen.

'I know you cannot gauge between the age gaps, David. I am not fifteen years old. Fifteen was an age I possessed a very long time ago. I am five hundred and thirty years old.'

'You can't be! You're so young', I protested, and Rasirine smiled gently.

'In my world, the signs of age come at one thousand, but not to worry, I still have many years before I actually age.'

It was so strange yet so magical that creatures had this amazing ability to live for such a long time. They were given the opportunity to see and explore the universe's treasures as many times as they wished and to develop such an advanced technology, allowing them to achieve seemingly impossible things.

I quickly returned the smile to Rasirine and then glimpsed out at the window and to continue with my silent thoughts. It was dark, and stars were sprayed everywhere—in the middle of space as we travelled past the planets, suns, moons, and galaxies.

I always knew there were other creatures out there. I had always wished for an extraterrestrial to come and find me, if not, I was determined to go and find them somehow. And now my dream had been realised. I was on the Neekan's spaceship, a real live spaceship. It was just like Rasirine had described it.

The spaceship was huge, containing gymnasiums, libraries, parks, eating houses with an immense variety of exotic and tasty foods. It was the most perfect thing that a human mind could ever conceive. When I was much younger and dreaming about adventures in the skies, travelling through the galaxies and freezing time with spaceships, my parents would always say in an unpleasant manner that I had a 'good story' to tell.

'It is forbidden for children to talk of these things', my mother would remind me in a stern voice. 'Ever since the incident with the outer space creatures, people have cut all communications with extraterrestrials.'

The incident was one of the worst things that happened of all time. It shook Earth and threatened its existence. All bases on the neighbouring planets and far across the various galaxies ceased to operate and finally were bombed. Any thought of advancing farther out into space was terminated, and anyone who attempted to speak of such ideas was labeled a futurist and was executed immediately.

Still, that never stopped me. They could torture me, hurt me, even kill me, but there was one thing they could not do and that was they could never take away my thoughts. Those were mine and only mine! So what if I wanted to think about travelling far and wide across the universe?

Then I interrupted my silent thoughts and ceased reminiscing by asking Rasirine, 'What is the key? Why am I the key? Why me? Why am I involved? You never got the chance to tell me. I am really curious to find out the answer to my questions.'

'Be patient, David', she responded in a calm voice.

'Be patient? How can I be patient when day and night, I am tormented by these thoughts? I do not even know what I am supposed to do. What do I need to do?'

I really wanted to be the best of help to her and her people. However, my internalised doubting feelings where telling me that I could not do it. Their world was so magical and extraordinarily advanced that I was left with little hope of believing in myself that I possessed any power to save Orchadia. I was constantly thinking that I would never be able to save their planet.

Rasirine insisted, 'You are the key, David. For many years, the prophecies have told that a young boy from Earth will be the key to the salvation of Orchadia. This boy has the power and will stop the burning of Orchadia.'

I was greatly startled as I was listening to Rasirine articulating the phrases.

Those words?! Those words were more than familiar to me! I had heard them every night as a child. I was afraid, unsettled, and felt extremely uncomfortable. I did not know what to do.

Words would not come out of my mouth for I feared the consequences of the mistaken phrase I may just speak.

In an urge to defend myself and hide my fear, I said, 'You must have the wrong boy! I am not that person. I cannot be! I cannot save Orchadia or whatever your place is called! I am not the one!'

Rasirine neared me in an attempt to pacify me, but I lashed out at her, 'Leave me alone! You are all freaks! Get me out of here!'

I ran up off my bed and banged my fists against the window. My head was spinning, and I ran to the door, but it closed before I reached the exit.

Rasirine mobilised herself against the wall of the spaceship, and mixed expressions of anger, pain, and rage appeared on her face. 'Do not dishonour my home! The prophecies must be definitely wrong! You, you are vermin!'

I froze to my standing position, hearing and seeing Rasirine reacting so angrily against my feelings of despair, and she continued, 'I thought you were different, but you are not! You are just like all the other humans in your race who care only about themselves! I hate you! I hate you so much!'

I could not resist replying, 'I never asked to be the key! I never wanted to do this! I thought you were kind and peaceful aliens! I thought you wanted to help us, but the story has changed now, and your only reason was that you wanted our help!'

Then I raised my voice in hopelessness. 'You wanted a backup planet in case your planet burned! That is not kindness, that is selfishness. We did not invade your planet. You came to our planet with ulterior motives!'

Rasirine retorted, 'Well, we have been studying your planet for years. Why is it a surprise to you? We obviously learnt from the best!'

She waited for a moment to see if I were going to respond and then came towards me and slapped me in the face, and then she ran back into the main room with tears flowing down her face.

The only person in the world that I would die willingly for, the princess of a world I longed to be a part of, now hated me. I hated myself. I hated the stupid words that came out of my mouth in fear and ignorance. She was right. I was the same as everyone else.

CHAPTER 7

I stayed in my room for hours on end, pacing up and down, thinking of ways on how to apologise and what to say. After many boring and tedious hours, Rasirine first knocked on my door and then opened it. 'Ras! Ras! I have been a horrible person. I am so sorry. Let me first explain. I was just so afraid. I did not know what to do.'

I paused for a second to regroup my thoughts so that I could provide a much more decent justification for my conduct and said, 'I was scared, I was confused. Please, please forgive me.'

I stood up and approached her. I wanted to hold her, but instead I reached out and took her hand in my hand and gazed into her eyes. I noticed her eyes were red, puffy, and still teary.

'What you said hurt me so much, David', Rasirine said in an unhappy tone of voice.

'I know, and I am really sorry, Rasirine.'

'I forgive you. I observed the strong emotions you felt. It is too much of a responsibility to save Orchadia. It demands a lot of self-reliance. You are the boy of the prophecy, David, and what I said about you being like everyone else was wrong.'

'We both said hurtful things, Rasirine.'

'Know that I love your people, and I will never hate you', she said and wiped her tears and embraced me; her skin's warmth made my heart beat so quickly. Hurting her was the worst thing I could have done.

'Now, let's go save your home', I said.

We walked into the main control room, and Rasirine said to her father, 'Father, we shall tell David about the secret part of the prophecy, and it is our duty to guide him in his journey'.

'Ras, please, let me address your father.' I turned to her father. 'Sir, I would like to know, what is the secret of the prophecy?'

'Call me Tarnak please', he said.

'Right, Tarnak, why shall you guide me? Will you not join me?'

'David, my boy, this journey is only for "the golden key". It is the golden key's journey, and since you are the golden key, you must complete it alone. On the day Orchadia burns, you will be alone. That is what the prophecies have told the youth of our nations for thousands of years.'

'With all due respect, sir, it is not what the prophecy says.'

Rasirine and Tarnak exchanged confused looks, and he asked me, 'And how would you know that son?' Before I got the chance to reply, he said, 'Think carefully how you put the words together. Do not insult the prophecies.'

I was mindful about what I wanted to say. I wanted to describe to them in every detail the dreams that haunted me every night. I wanted to tell them about this strange woman visiting me in my sleep.

However, something was holding me back, but I managed to utter three words: 'My recurring dreams'.

Rasirine and Tarnak gasped. 'The rumors were true then!' Rasirine exclaimed.

'Tell me, son, do you know who was sending you the frightening dreams?' Tarnak asked.

'No, I do not know, sir, who that person is. All I know is that this strange but beautiful woman was calling out all these strange names that had no meaning to me, and she would constantly talk about a date that I cannot recall.'

'She was beautiful, you say?' confirmed Tarnak.

'Yes!'

'I presume it is the Abbess Rheydaya, the wisest and the youngest priestess of the prophets. What do you think, Rasirine?'

Rasirine did not answer, but she asked me, 'Were you ever told about a book?'

'A book? Let me think.' I struggled to remember. 'I . . . I think I recall something, but it is not very clear.'

'Perhaps when you sleep, you might be able to give a chance to the recurring dreams to pay a visit again in your head. This time, try and retain the name of the book.'

'The dreams evolve very fast, sir, and I am not sure if I would be able to remember much.'

'I will ask Rasirine to make you some tea from the Orchadian mountains. This tea will help you fall asleep.'

I wondered how Sir Tarnak expected me to instantly have those same recurring dreams by just falling asleep. It has been some years now that I have not had those recurring dreams.

Nevertheless, I tried to focus on the dreams and the messages whilst I was awake, but I was not able to remember anything. I kept replaying the messages in my head and the scattered phrases the priestess was mumbling. Nothing helped me to decode the message.

Rasirine brought me some of the blue tea in a silver saucer. I drank it, and within a few minutes, I felt myself falling asleep.

'My child, you have been brought to Orchadia by your friend Rasirine and her father. They knew these days were to come, and now they have arrived. I shall tell you of the book, for a man as wise as you knew to tell them about your dreams, the sole intention I had of appearing in them.'

'Who are you?'

'Your feelings of trust for your friend and her father have been transmitted to me. It is a virtue that many souls do not posse. Given your character traits, it is evident that you must know about the book.'

'What is the name of the book, ma'am?'

'The book has been kept in a secret place, and all are under the impression that it has been lost for many centuries.'

'Does that mean I can never have possession of the book?'

'No! Of course not! It is now your task to find the book, but you need to know the title and the name of the book.'

'I was told to make sure that I get to remember the title of the book. Who knows the title of the book? How can I find out its name?'

'No one knows the name of the book but me. I got to know about the book's title by the Neekan elders who wrote the book. And the only way the title was allowed to be passed on was through the priests and priestesses.'

'Where is the book hidden? What is the secret place?'

'The secrets of Orchadia are buried deep in the sands of your planet Earth. The book has instructions on how the universe can be saved. You do not have much time for when Orchadia, burns the rest of the cosmos shall also burn and a paradox of death and hate shall prevail everywhere.'

'Priestess, I am begging you with all my might to please hurry and tell me the name of the book!'

'I shall tell you the name of the book, but first I must warn you. Beware, for when you start this journey, danger of all kind shall follow. War, fire, destruction, anger, despair, violence, and death shall come to you.'

'So be it, ma'am! I promised my friend that I will do whatever it takes to save their world and the universe.'

'You must finish this mission, boy, and what I mean by this is that you must complete what you will begin because after the war, the Neekan elders will be waiting for you with the book.'

'Where shall I find the Neekan elders? Shall I search for them in Orchadia?'

'Do not go to the Neekan elders till the war is over for it is your duty, David Christopher Alexander Matthew Robert Harrison, to save the universe. And without the Neekan's freedom, the universe cannot be saved.'

I woke up abruptly. I opened my eyes and saw Tarnak and Rasirine's face filled with hope, and I quickly began retelling them of my so-vivid dream.

'It has been thus proven. You shall find *The Secrets of Orchadia* immediately.'

'Father, I will go with David.'

This was not going to be easy for either of us, but I wanted Rasirine to be with me.

'When do we leave, David?' she asked me.

'In ten minutes, Rasirine'

'Get your battle armour', Tarnak called after her.

He turned to me and said, 'Let me show you something of great value to my family. Follow me.'

Tarnak led me across the hallway of the spaceship to a small cabinet, which had a large golden lock on the outside inscribed with two golden symbols.

'This is the coat of arms for my family, David. This armour has stayed in my family for over forty thousand years and has a layer of protection against evil spirits. I am handing it over to you. Take good care of it as you shall need it soon.'

'Are you confident, sir, that I am worthy of such honour?'

'Rasirine has told me of your efforts against the slavery of my people by your people. When you return, your people shall all be against you. Fight for your beliefs, son. Fight with my people to save Orchadia and the universe. Fight with my daughter's assistance because it is part of her duty too, as a princess of Orchadia, to save our planet and the galaxies.'

I bowed to Sir Tarnak with respect after receiving the armour.

Tarnak has now become the father I never got to see, for my father was murdered many years ago in the underground service for supporting the Neekans. He died from sufferance.

I tried not to think about my father's death, but my mother was constantly telling me of how special he was despite the fact that he was always angry and violent. I could not understand why my mother was trying to instill in me some liking for my father.

Then I turned around and responded to Tarnak. 'I will, sir.'

Rasirine entered back into the main hall, all prepared for the battle.

'Are you both ready?' Tarnak asked.

'Yes!' we both responded in unison.

CHAPTER 8

Going through the teleport with the electron beams was a superb feeling. Travelling through the waves of the beam felt like being slightly stretched with a pleasant sensation running through my body and through my joints to the point where for a second it felt like my joints were going to be dislocated.

Rasirine and I landed back to my house in our normal rematerialised Neekan and human state respectively.

The police, with the aid of the military force, was waiting for us. They were well prepared and equipped with their sophisticated weapons for the attack.

My home was surrounded by numerous flightmobiles. Rasirine and I remained in the main area of the house, standing back to back, observing both sides of the house. Then we heard loud repetitive kicks on the front door.

The door was knocked down, and three policemen entered the house. We instantly directed our laser beams to the policemen and killed them. With a swift jump, I turned to the right and Rasirine to the left, aiming at the rest of the soldiers appearing one by one on either side of the house.

Rasirine was a real fighter but impulsive and impatient at times, so she yelled out, 'Come on, powerful humans, attempt to shoot us with your weak weapons. I cannot wait for the painful death that you are trying to inflict upon us!' And aimed with her laser gun at the ceiling, releasing a short beam.

Fragments of the ceiling were hanging from where she had shot the beam.

'Oh, look, Ras, there is a tall man hiding behind some guards!'

'Why is he here? What does he want?'

'This is the type of society we live in, Rasirine. One leads and the rest follow.'

'What do you mean, David?'

The conversation with Rasirine at this time had to be limited. I chose not to respond and just whisper, 'Shhhh! The rich humans support the government in our world, Rasirine.'

'I still do not understand.'

'Rasirine, most humans have mental and emotional problems. My father was one of them. He had huge complexities that I cannot explain to you now.'

'You do not like your father, do you?'

'It does not really matter now because he is dead. But strangely enough, it feels like he is haunting me.'

For a few minutes, everything came to a stand. No policemen, no soldiers were attempting to invade the house.

Rasirine asked, 'What is happening, David?'

'Do not move. Stay with your feet planted on the ground, ready to attack.'

The tall man spoke through the megaphone, a devise which made his voice ten times louder.

He asked, 'Whose side are you on, David?'

Rasirine prompted me, 'Answer him'.

I replied in anger, 'Definitely not on the side of the feuding races'.

'What are you trying to say, David?'

'You know what I mean, whoever you may be!' And there was a pregnant pause.

'Your father was a human. Are you saying that you do not like your father?'

'That is none of your business. I loved my father, but he instead loved money more than me. The Neekans have been loyal to me, and they appreciate me for what I am. I made a promise to help them even if it is going to cost my life.'

'We are more advanced than them, David! Join forces with us. Come back to us! We have better technology than the Neekans.'

'What, the fancy flightmobiles, spacemansions, submarinegrams? Or the rockets that constantly travel back and forth to the moon and the neighbouring galaxies?'

'Yes, David! And do not scorn our technology because it took us humans several hundreds of years of research and hard work to reach where we are now. This is your last chance to join forces with us.'

I turned to Rasirine and said, 'This is our affluent and insincere human society, Rasirine. Well, the time has come.'

'David, this man seems to pose great emotional power and intelligence over the other humans.'

I laughed and whispered, 'If I join forces with the humans now, they will kill me.'

Rasirine released a deep laugh like that of a villain, which I somehow liked. Why? I do not know? All I know is that it gave me strength.

'Back away and leave now. Otherwise, war will start', Rasirine said in a threatening voice.

'The time has come to rise up against the slavery of the Neekans and fight every man and woman who tries to stop us. The world is changing, sir. Now it is us that give you the opportunity to either join us or die. Make your choice.'

David was so proud of Rasirine. He swerved through the window and observed that all who were armed took aim at the house, and a few seconds later, they started shooting bullets of uncountable number.

'Keep shooting, boys!' Rasirine said in determination.

'Come on, waste all your bullets! It will make killing you much easier!'

I had never seen Rasirine like this before. She was keeping me constantly on my toes. The feeling of strength and power was now even more accentuated in me. I aimed towards the shooters and shot a few on the arm and many on the legs, leaving many gaping holes on their body via the laser beam.

Cries of pain were filling the surroundings. The military and the police ceased fire and threw their weapons down. They wanted a truce. They stood with their hands up and backed away slowly. The ones with wounds limped towards their escape so as not to sustain any more injuries from out laser beam guns.

'We never meant to enslave you, David!' the tall man uttered in a fearful tone of voice.

'You did not? Oh, I am sorry! Then how about we all hold hands and sing Kumbayah?'

'Please accept our apology. We can arrange a meeting so as to sign a new treaty of partnership that will never be revoked. We can work together, humans and Neekans. I promise. We are all very sorry. It was a mistake to commence war with the faraway galaxies. The universe does not belong to us.'

Before the tall man could say anything, Rasirine cut him off and walked right near him. She placed the gun near his head. Her voice was now trembling with anger, and in an exasperated breath she spoke. 'The words *sorry*, *promise*, *loyalty*, and *friendship* mean nothing to you. They are just sounds coming out of your mouth! It is final. War shall begin today. Be prepared for what is coming, for it is your mind and the minds of power-hungry humans that caused this.'

The tall man stared at Rasirine with a disorientated look. Rasirine backed away with caution and entered the house safely. The tall man ordered his men to back off.

'Ras, you are the strength I lacked. We will fight them together.' As the words left my mouth, the camera in our apartment swiveled and focused on us.

'Ouch!' Rasirine gasped.

Blood was trickling down her hand. When I rotated my body to attend to her wrist, a sharp piercing pain shot me in the right wrist.

'What is happening!?' Rasirine cried out to me.

'Stay still, Rasirine.'

I quickly ran to the medicine cupboard and pulled out some bandages. I returned to Rasirine and asked her to give me her hand so that I can bandage it. The blood had stopped, and I observed a thick red line marking a symbol. I looked back to my wrist, and the identical symbol was on mine too.

It was a large red *X*, which then turned black in colour with an arrow passing through the middle. Underneath the symbol there was writing: 'The mark of the Neekan fighters.'

Rasirine and I exchanged looks. We compared the two marks, and upon realising how identical they were, we contacted our other Neekan friends. All of them had the same mark.

'Ras, tell everyone that the revolution begins in seven hours and for all to be at their posts. Today is the day we fight for the universe!'

CHAPTER 9

Rasirine and I planned our attack positions by drawing a diagram on contactogram. We were at the main building where humans segregate for major meetings and decision making. We marked the humans' meeting room with a light wave.

The proposal was to dive straight into the humans' office and catch them by ultimate surprise. The steps were to shoot and kill those who attempted to hurt us but those who would show remorse we would set free. Then we would take two as hostages to trade. We would free the hostages only in exchange for the Neekans' freedom.

Rasirine asked, 'Where did you get this wisdom, David? You have not even found the book *The Secrets of Orchadia.*'

Though this had no connection to finding the book *The Secrets of Orchadia*, I received the wisdom from the abbess of the prophets.

'Rasirine, you and I defeated the first blockage fate had placed in our way, hand in hand. So do not be afraid. I presume it is my father's communication interfering with my actions from the world of the dead.'

'I don't think we should take two of them as hostages, David. Just rethink, what if they take one of our people as hostage too?'

At that moment, I felt my father's presence.

'Rasirine, did you see my dad?' Rasirine stopped writing and looked at me as if I was losing my mental stability.

'I will check the security wavelength cameras', she said and bolted to my computer to hack into the building's camera footage. Some old events recorded on the camera were showing my father. I asked Rasirine to come closer.

'Come and see my father, Rasirine. Look at him walking into the house and getting captured by the guards.'

'They have tied him down. Why? How?'

'I do not understand, Rasirine. Look, they are constantly questioning him about me.'

'I can hear that. Your father seems exhausted. But look, David! He is not there anymore. Your father is no longer in the room. Where has he gone?'

I looked closely at the cameras. 'The guards used electric current to distort the recording waves.'

'Look, David! This is strange. Your father appears again.'

For a moment, I was lost in my sweeping thoughts. Rasirine's voice interrupted my silent thinking, and I looked at the cameras again. I saw my father slowing dying as the guards tortured him. It was all the fault of my own stupid head.

'Rasirine, you know that I never liked my father. I never agreed with him, and I resented him deeply for selling out my mother.'

'Do not feel bad about the way you felt for your father. You do not need to explain. It is justifiable since he betrayed your mother's trust.'

'You know, Rasirine, the fact that he was not telling the guards my whereabouts, it was not because he did not want them to find me. It was because he never knew where I was. He considered me lost. You could see from the expression in his eyes that he was not at all sad that I was lost.'

'Why do you feel this way about your father, David?'

'My whole life, I had felt unwanted and unloved by him. Every word that came out of his mouth made me loathe him more and more till a wrath of unimaginable strength escaped from my body and attacked everything I saw in front of me. I became brutal. My father, my own father, had caused so much pain to me my whole life. He murdered my mother, and now he was haunting me.'

'But you are his child, how could he feel this way about you?'

'Rasirine, you do not understand. He was telling me that I was interfering with his plans all the time, and he did not like that. I was a burden to him. He would find any possible excuse not to help me or spend time with me. Why do you think I was so happy to meet up with you, Glaron, and Kirlan every afternoon after school?'

'It is so sad, David. Now I understand why you are so fearless. You do not even care for your life. Your strength is built from unhappy encounters with your father. I can feel your human heart beats for longing for some warmth and understanding. I care about you, David, and I want you to become the prince of Orchadia. My father is very fond of you, but he does not like your people.'

'Rasirine, I do not seek revenge on my people. However, I do not like the pain and the slavery that my people are causing your people. I somehow feel protected and invincible by the power drawn from the Neekans. I want to save your planet. Orchadia is in my heart.'

Rasirine looked at me and asked, 'What is happiness like in your world, David?'

'For me, Rasirine, it is a compelling journey with your most loved ones.'

I did not want Rasirine to know that it was mortifying having my father in my thoughts. I wanted him to suffer and to writhe in the pain that he had caused me all these years. Even dead, he was hindering my progress into achieving what I was meant to achieve.

Many times, I wanted to explain to her that I did not set out to win against my fellow humans. I did not want that. My belief was to teach the two races, both humans and Neekans, to start living together. I wanted to find brilliant ways to defy evil forces and to save Orchadia and the universe. I had this conviction that every step was taking me closer to the day.

CHAPTER 10

I gathered the weapons and stacked them on the side, ready to take them with us. Then I called Glaron and organised to meet him with Rasirine outside the main building.

I called out to Rasirine, 'Are you ready, Ras?'

'Just getting a few beams ready for the laser guns. Is Glaron armed?'

'No, we are going to supply him with the beams.'

'Let's go start the war that will rock the world for eons to come.'

Rasirine and I headed towards the main building. We walked for about half an hour, and then before we approached the main entrance of the building, I tried to communicate with Glaron from the intercom.

'Glaron, where are you? We are here.' There was no response.

'Glaron, hello, helloooo! Are you on the roof?' I whispered into the intercom and waited for a response from Glaron. I checked if the intercom was damaged, but it seemed to be working fine.

I tried once more. 'Glaron, David here. What are you doing!?' He still would not respond. Then there was the incoming beep.

'Yes, yes, David, relax, I am on the roof trying to locate the window.'

'Turn south and walk five steps towards the small passage. Once you cross the passage, you will see the window.'

'OK, I think I can see the window. It is screwed on quite tight. Give me three minutes and I will have it opened nicely without any scratches and marks of forced entrance.'

Glaron was slow at times and very stubborn, but he was the most efficient hacker. I had a lot of trust in him when a task was given to him to carry out. This is why I trusted him with my life. Glaron was one of my closest Neekan friends.

'Done!' Glaron responded.

We now had seven minutes to get inside.

'Ras, you go from the back door. There will be a guard pacing up and down. If he stops you and asks why you are there, you show him this ID.'

'What is this ID for?'

'You must pretend to be the building's cleaner and move as naturally as you can. Do not speak to anyone. Do you understand?'

'Yes, David, I do understand. How long do we have?'

'We have approximately five minutes. Let's synchronise our watches. What is the time on your watch?'

'Now, it is eighteen minutes past eight, right?'

'Correct! At twenty-three minutes past eight, Rasirine, you must break open the door of the main chamber and point the gun directly to the chairperson. He is wearing a black suit with a white shirt and a red tie. He is the only one who wears the red tie. The other delegates wear a blue tie.'

'Where would Glaron be?'

'Glaron will be right behind you with a rope.' I had to make sure that Glaron was listening via the intercom device too. 'You got that too, Glaron?'

'Yes, David, I am listening in too.'

'Glaron, you must lower yourself silently, and when Rasirine breaks in, cut the rope and group off one section of the members. I will follow in shortly. Anyone who resists is your target. Shoot to kill.'

I stopped the intercom and moved closer to Rasirine. 'See you on the other side, Ras.'

With a nod, she walked off, headed towards her mission silently as a cautious cat to catch its prey. Rasirine disappeared in the darkness.

I squatted down and took a few hesitant steps towards the main entrance. I waited a few seconds hidden beside the fence wall before I could charge in and make a strong appearance. Then I stood up and climbed over the fence and into the lavish gardens.

I disabled the main frame of the alarm system and made my way through the grounds. When I reached the seemingly deserted door, two large security officers took out their guns and aimed them at me.

'Move any farther and we will shoot.'

I honestly had enough for one day. Without any words, I grinned at them, chuckled, and shot them. Their bodies collapsed on the ground. I burst through the doors, and the alarms loudly blasted through every speaker.

'Intruder! Intruder!' the alarms continuously blared.

I made a break for the main chamber. It seemed too easy. Right before I shot the door handle, a laser maze lined the hallway. I managed to tightly squeeze between the burning lasers. I had two minutes left.

I could hear some faint talking coming my way. I slid through the first layer, and then I pushed my hand through a gap between the two laser lines and moved my body in a snake-like movement through the rest of the laser lines.

When I reached the door, another three security guards encountered me from the side hallways. I had forty-six seconds remaining. I definitely was not going to mess it up now.

With a point of my laser, I stop them straight in the eyes.

'Get out of my way!' I roared.

The guards looked at my laser beam and froze. They took a step back and retreated to hide in one of the adjacent rooms.

I used my gun to shoot the lock of the chambers once, twice; still, it would not dismantle. I thought for a moment that I did not have time for this. I quickly tested the material of the metal with my scanner. It gave me the result of strengthened steel.

Of course, how did I not think about it? I immediately increased the level of power on my laser gun to maximum, which burnt the door lock straight off its hinges.

'Hello, gentlemen! We meet again. Do you have some scones? I am feeling quite hungry. Oh yes, do not worry yourselves. I am not going to hurt you. All I want from you is to give orders to free all the Neekans.'

I saw Rasirine charging in too and Glaron following behind.

'Ras, Glaron, now!'

The whole room had this deafening silence. The members were afraid and shocked. The only sound that was bouncing in the chambers was the sound waves of my angry voice. I looked at Rasirine and Glaron.

'We did the right thing!'

One of the members decided to speak. It was a short woman with greyish hair who looked like she was part of the advisory team. She took a hesitant step forward, and she looked quite frightened, but she managed to ask, 'Why do you support them, boy? Do you know that they came to our planet Earth in search for a book? They want to end our world.'

'No they do not, madam! You are completely wrong. I have grown up with the Neekans. All they want is to find the book *The Secrets of Orchadia*. The reason being their planet in their galaxy is going to burn. If their planet gets destroyed, then the rest of the universe will be destroyed too.'

'Where are they going to find their book? Their supposed scientists, as they address themselves, started excavating our countries and leaving holes deep as the ocean. They have invaded us. They have threatened us that if we do not let them find their book, it would be the end of the world! We are only trying to protect the human race.'

I couldn't believe what I was hearing.

With my feet planted apart on the floor and having one hand rested by my side on my hip and with my other hand pointing the laser gun at them, I asked, 'Oh, and in order to avenge the Neekans. you keep them captive and then enslave them. Is this the human way, madam? What is your name, madam if I may ask?'

'I am Lady Maria De Kristina Lorentiana.'

'I am David, madam. Let me ask you this question. Are you implying that your delegates and your members meet secretly to decide the future of the universe?'

'No! We are having these meetings to save our planet Earth, Mr. David. What would you have done if you were in our position?'

'The Neekans are superior extraterrestrial beings than us. I have been to their galaxy and back. I know what they are all about. They have a rare quality of technology and knowledge and ability to travel back and forth in time. They have given humans the opportunity to cooperate with them in order to save their planet Orchadia and the universe. Instead, you have disregarded their knowledge and plea.'

Rasirine interrupted me. 'With all respect, David, I really do not think we have much more time left. We need to proceed fast.'

'I know, Rasirine, but let's give these members another chance to cooperate with us.'

I looked at the members and asked, 'Who has the Neekans' mark?'

No one moved or replied. Then I asked again, 'Those who have the mark, step forward. You can come with us, and we will keep you safe.

The rest may get the mark now if you wish and join forces with us. Otherwise, stay with the unmarked men and women. You will be viewed as those who have betrayed a race that came to save you and the universe. Do so and be prepared to face your imminent death.'

First, two women stepped forward, and then the rest of the men except for one. I did not know for certain why he did not want to get the mark. However, I did not persist with him, but I asked the rest, 'Do you really want to join forces with us?'

'Yes, we do', one of them spoke on behalf of their team.

Glaron was standing dumbfounded, not believing what he was hearing.

'Get the mark, Glaron, from your people immediately!'

In the meantime, I wanted to make sure of their intentions and questioned them again. 'Is it because you realise that it is for the salvation of the universe or because you are in a terrified state of mind now?'

Glaron stopped, turned around, and said, 'I have been around humans long enough to know when they are making up something, David. They really want to help, but they are also afraid.'

'Afraid of what? Do not tell me of us?' I spoke back to Glaron with discontent.

'Oh, David, do you not know that your people are afraid of death? They have the will power to fight, but they do not want to die.'

'Get the mark, Glaron. I have faith in my race too. I have told you before that not all of them are bad.'

All of the members got the mark, even the one who was hesitant and remained behind, he stepped forward and got the mark also. Rasirine took out a can of a rainbow-coloured spray paint and sprayed, 'The revolution has begun!'

A sudden explosion, which was set up as a defense mechanism and protection for the building, shot Rasirine, Glaron, and me ten metres away to the nearby Hover Park.

As we regained strength, we stood up, regrouped, and quickly looked around to see if there were any of the members there too. But we did not see anyone.

Rasirine said that all the delegates were instantly killed as a group since they were standing all together in one spot. The delegates were right next to the room where the explosion happened and simultaneously filled the rooms with poisonous gases.

Rasirine called out in desperation that we did not have much more time. She urged us to move quickly as the bodies of the men and women were falling out of the building in their attempt to jump out of the windows to escape the poisonous gases. Unfortunately, the bodies, one after the other, met the ground in a horrific splash with blood spurting everywhere.

For a moment, I was immobilised with the tragic event unfolding before my eyes, and my mind fled back to an incident that happened many centuries ago with the twin towers in the greatest country of the world. The whole planet mourned this catastrophe.

This country helped the nations to keep their peace and assisted many countries to regain their independence. My favourite president was President Lincoln, who had great tenacity.

Glaron's voice interrupted my thoughts by yelling out, 'Off to the central intelligence agency to see what is happening there!'

Rasirine insisted to first attack the broadcasting centres and destroy the communication facilities. I just looked at her. I was so distraught and saddened by the incident, seeing my fellow humans dying in such a horrific way.

I asked both Glaron and Rasirine to cease fighting and to go back home. I had seen enough pain unfolding before me. I was feeling already emotionally low, and every hope in me for a better and safer world and universe was getting dimmer. I was extremely discouraged and thought that there must be a better way to fulfill this mission.

Rasirine and Glaron looked puzzled.

Glaron could not believe that I was starting to give up.

'Are you okay, buddy?' he asked me.

'I was the cause of this atrocious image that we all saw. I killed my own people, and you are asking me if I am all right? Well, no! I am really not.'

Glaron said that it would be a good idea to enter the flightmobile and return home.

CHAPTER 11

'Morning, David, how are you feeling today?'

'Good morning, Ras. I am feeling better, but where is Glaron?'

'He slept in the basement of the house.'

'Why? What happened?'

'You were not feeling the best after the tragic incident at the main building, and when we got home, you were both mentally and emotionally exhausted, so you fell asleep on the couch. Glaron did not want to disturb you, so he went and slept in the basement.'

'I am so sorry about last night . . . I just felt so weak . . .'

'Save your breath. I know how you felt. You felt guilty and miserable, but do not worry about that! Look on the news!'

I turned on the hologram, and a faint beeping noise connected me to the broadcasting services.

'The chairman and the chamber members were found dead inside the building during their meeting yesterday. A witness said he saw three people leaving the building wearing dark clothing. One of them was a female with a turquoise skin, presuming a Neekan. Further, the investigating team observed a strange symbol marked on the wrists of the members which resembled the "mark" of the enslaved Neekans. The wall was inscribed: "The revolution has begun!"'

I was taken aback with the announcement and especially when a warning was given out to all humans to remain in their homes, armed to protect their families from the Neekans.

I called out to Rasirine whilst she was cooking breakfast for Glaron. 'Rasirine, you have alarmed the humans with your rainbow phrase. They are all terrified now.'

For a strange reason Rasirine could not contain herself and launched this huge and continuous laughter. I approached her and reminded her that what she did was uncalled for.

Rasirine replied, 'Come on, David, please do not take things so seriously. I was bored. I did not think that the rainbow-coloured phrase will alarm humans to this extent.'

Glaron, in a drained and fearful tone of voice, said, 'The police have been investigating?'

'Of course they are investigating', I said in mouthfuls of food. 'Do you think they would not be concerned about the bodies lying everywhere?'

'We did not stop all broadcasting communication as Rasirine suggested, did we? And the cameras, we did not destroy them?'

Rasirine, Glaron, and I all looked at each other with fear. Then Glaron pointed at the cameras above. We knew that my home was bugged.

'Run!' Glaron yelled. Rasirine and I picked up our weapons and bolted out of the house as fast as we could. Glaron caught up with us at a later stage, handing us our fake IDs.

CHAPTER 12

We headed towards the electricity generators. We thought for hours seriously that it was the best approach. If we were to cut off all power, there would be no need to kill any more humans in order to complete our mission.

We knew that we were definitely going to encounter some resistance, but it would be much easier to fight humans if there was no electricity.

'Are you ready to cut off the power?' Rasirine asked.

'No!' and I looked at Glaron. 'Are you sure, Glaron, that it is a good idea?'

'Yes, David. We have thought about it for hours. Your people depend on electricity. Everything operates with electricity in your planet. They will not be able to resist us.'

I was a little hesitant. The thought that everything was going to collapse once the general supply of power was going to be terminated was holding me back.

Rasirine insisted. 'This is it, David, if this plan fails, we are all dead—planet Earth and universe.'

'I won't fail, Rasirine! One, two, three—out! All shutdown. There you are!'

Glaron neared me and gave me a strong pat on my back.

'The whole world has turned off now. The main electricity generator and the base supplying electricity to the whole planet have irreparable damage. Let the war begin.'

We had arranged with all the Neekans to meet here in the countryside of England tonight for the start of the war. We would spread into the city and free first all the Neekan slaves. Wherever we were, our approach was centre minded. We all had to reach the centre. No matter what obstacles were thrown in our way.

'Promise me one thing, Ras', I asked her as I looked into her large green eyes.

'Promise me, if I am stuck or taken, you will continue on without me. You must find the book! This is my mission, your mission, our mission.'

Rasirine held me tight in her embrace. 'I do not want to ever leave you. I would rather watch the world burn with you in my arms rather than save it without you to see it', she said crying.

'I want our baby to see us save it together', Rasirine said.

'Our baby?' I asked.

'Yes, David, I am expecting our Neekan and human baby.'

I froze as the words were unfolding out of Rasirine's mouth. I did not know whether to be happy or sad. The feeling of joy overtook and spread inside me like a blazing fire.

Rasirine stood there looking at me. For a fleeting moment, she observed a star and said, 'Look at that beautiful shooting star. It looks like it is coming straight towards us'.

'Funny you say that, Ras, because I thought the exact same thing.'
'Did you see the red hurtling ball of fire speeding towards us?'
'Yes, I did. I think it landed a few lightyears away from our planet.'

'Look, there is another hurtling red star approaching us with a higher speed. It is coming directly towards us this time. What is it, David?'

When the red hurtling object landed not far away from where we were standing, it was glowing even redder. I ran towards it with Rasirine running after me. This strange object was on fire, but there were no flames. I went closer to examine it. As I was observing its oddly symmetrical shape, I noticed it had the number four on the side of it. Then the number changed to three and a few seconds later to one.

Rasirine and I panicked and started running away from it. Within few seconds, it exploded and left a large gaping hole in the ground.

'David! Look, there are more coming from the skies!' Rasirine cried out.

'No, they are not falling from the sky. They are coming from those tanks.'

They had found us.

Rasirine lifted her arm and grabbed my hand, squeezing it so tightly that I thought my hand was going to fall off. Then she said, 'I have reserve charge in my teleport. We will transport to our starting place by distorting time. Just give me fifty seconds. I need to fight them back before we take off.'

I could hardly understand what Rasirine was doing when there were tanks shooting explosive grenades every second and she wanted fifty seconds to fight them back. She pulled out a device, which in two seconds inflated something that looked like an atomic bomb.

'How on Earth did you get that!?' I inquired hastily.

'I made sure to outsource myself with this device when you were rude to me. I thought I had to blow you up.'

I was knocked over with Rasirine's remark. I did not expect such a response.

She looked at me and hastily said, 'Oh, wipe that look off your face! I knew we were going to war, so I made some weapons'.

'What are you doing, Rasirine? Stop! You cannot do this!'

'Get out of the way!' And she swung her arm with such unbelievable speed that no human force would have been able to prevent her from throwing the bomb directly in the path of the tanks.

Rasirine yelled out, 'David, twenty seconds and we have two seconds before the bomb goes. We must teleport now!'

Fireball grenades were falling all around us. A spark from one lit a fire on the tall grass. Watching the fire grow as we ran to a safe place to teleport, the heat was growing insufferable. It spread all over the grass within seconds, stopping just before us as we managed to reach and lean against our flightmobile to teleport. Everything went black.

I woke up after a few moments lightheaded and tired.

'You have always been really bad at geography, have you not, David?' Rasirine remarked.

'Yes, since we distort time through teleporting, I tend to lose all orientation from planet Earth. Where are we, Ras?'

My head was spinning, and I felt nauseous as I tried to stand up and walk towards Rasirine. I fell back down without being able to control my balance and fell and hurt my leg. The pain was so sharp to the point where it directed my focus to the burnt bone piercing the skin. My leg was swimming in blood. Blood was everywhere. Rasirine ran towards my screams of agony and fell down beside me.

'Your leg got burnt at the fire just before we teleported. Oh, David! Your leg is so badly hurt.' She reached in her bag and pulled out a bandage. She started bandaging my leg and at one instance, she stopped to warn me, 'This is going to hurt you, David, but I need to push the bone back into its place. It is for your own good'.

The pain was unbearable as she pushed the bone back into its place. In the darkness, my wails sounded off the hills. I could not bear the pain, and in desperation, I asked Rasirine to use her powers to heal my leg.

CHAPTER 13

Rasirine used her Neekan healing powers to heal my leg, and within a few minutes, it was back to normal. My human egotism got in the way, stubbornly tolerating the excruciating pain and thinking that I was able to heal in the 'normal' human way.

Rasirine had positioned next to the table a sophisticated glass machine that was able to scan through the universe all the planets and even Earth. Through this glass machine with magnetic waves, which were translated into icons, I was able to see what was happening on planet Earth.

At first I saw a small light flicker and then people running through flames.

'See that, Ras?' I said fearfully. 'That is our first target, Ras.'

'Not yet', she said in a discontented manner.

'We are not ready to attack. You are not ready. Tonight, we sleep on this planet.'

'What is this planet called, Ras?'

'The Neekans call it Zeng.'

'Does it mean anything?' I asked her in impatient curiosity.

'No, not really, the only explanation that I can think of is that planet Zeng is "Zeng years" away from Orchadia. Probably this is the most human logical explanation that I can give you so you will understand.' Then she pointed out, 'I am kind of feeling tired'.

It was apparent that she was exhausted. Retreating to her bed was her salvation. She desperately wanted to recharge her cosmic energy. She consumed a lot of power by healing my broken leg and travelling across the universe and distorting time.

'Yes, Rasirine, go to bed. Thank you very much for helping me and bandaging my leg.'

I remained outside looking at the skies and the stars. I was reminiscing of my childhood years. I recalled sitting outside on the verandah, gazing at the skies with my mother. Mother and I spent many nights looking, in a serene silence, at the stars and wondering whether other life existed in those faraway shining diamonds.

I saw some clouds drifting silently across the sky and I begun giving the clouds names. *That one looks like a flower*, I was thinking. The one next to the 'flower' cloud looked like a cat. I lay there, tranquil for hours, watching the night passing by silently, waiting for the signs of the early dawn. Finally, sleepiness made its way through the hollow and cavernous cavity embedded in my brain. I do not recall precisely at what time I fell asleep.

I was woken up by Rasirine's sweet voice. 'David, wake up. It is nearly midday.'

I jumped out of bed like a spring. Rasirine woke me up from an ugly dream. I envisioned that I was in the war and the same terror-striking events were unfolding before my presence. I saw my body lying lifeless on the ground next to a weeping Rasirine.

I told Rasirine about my dream and she said, 'I heard you crying whilst you were asleep, and you were mumbling some words that I could not make sense of.'

'In my dream, I saw a man losing both his legs and a tank going over him. I screamed from the top of my lungs, but the soldier driving the tank could not hear me. I broke down in tears. Tears were running down my face, but my eyes would not open. They were cemented shut with a fear so strong and terrible. I suddenly felt cold, a cold that chilled straight to the bone, when you came and woke me up, Ras.'

'David, you are exhausted too. Come on, eat up and drink some blue tea. I have prepared some eggs for you too. In Orchadia, we do not cook birds' eggs for breakfast.'

The eggs were cooked to perfection. She was a better cook than so many other humans.

When I finished eating my fried eggs and drunk my tea, Rasirine and I assembled our gear quickly, and we got back to our seats and teleported back to Earth. We did not want to go back to my house because definitely, my people had surveillance. Neither was it safe to stay in one place for too long.

As we walked into town, we came face-to-face with destroyed homes, burnt parks, half-demolished buildings, and civilians starving and begging for some food and shelter. We were getting into the colder months of the year on planet Earth.

CHAPTER 14

Rasirine and I were walking down the streets, observing the remains of the destroyed buildings. As we were casually standing in the main square, a policeman stopped us and asked for our identity proof. 'What are your names please?'

We produced our IDs and handed them over to him. The policeman observed the IDs for five seconds, and then he asked, 'Is there anything wrong with your cards?'

Rasirine looked at me, wondering what was wrong with our cards.

I responded to the policeman, 'No, sir, our cards are fine'.

The policeman looked at Rasirine and asked for her to state her name.

'My name, sir, is Maria Richards'. And then he asked me.

'Jack Richards, sir.'

The policeman moved a few steps away from us and talked on his intercom device to his headquarters to verify the information given to him about our identity. Then he returned to us and said, 'I would like to draw your attention to the fact that our people are desperate at this stage for all the destruction that has taken place in the past few days. Please refrain from any violence or reacting back to any provocation.'

I was happy that Rasirine and I were able to disguise our identity.

The policeman looked at me and said, 'You have to be very careful, Mr. Richards, parading with a Neekan wife down the streets of this city.'

'You are legally married, right?' he questioned with an unpleasant tone of voice.

'Yes, sir, do you have a problem with that?' I retaliated.

Rasirine got offended and splurged out to the policeman. 'Next time we want to make a decision about affirming our love, we will ask you, sir.'

The policeman looked at Rasirine and said, 'Madam, please keep your voice down and do not attempt to raise your voice at me again.'

Rasirine and I shot him a dirty look.

We did not appreciate the way he was addressing us, and especially Rasirine for she was a Neekan. We left the policeman and paced down the street, arriving at a small eating in shop that was selling three different dishes of pasta.

'I am getting hungry, Ras. What do you think of getting a pasta dish?'

'Yes, that is fine, David. I am not particularly hungry, but I will keep you company.'

We entered the small shop, and as we made ourselves comfortable sitting at the back of the room, so as to not attract any further attention from anyone else, a robot handed us the menu from which we ordered some pasta dish to share.

The few people that were sitting in the eatery suddenly stopped talking and looked at us as we walked in. They did not resume their casual conversations for quite some time, which made Rasirine uncomfortable and self-conscious.

'Ras, do not take them seriously. You can see that they have pain, suffering, and violence painted in their looks? They are just like us.'

Rasirine refused to understand and instead she shot me an angry look. She immediately pulled out of her bag a pair of thick black sunglasses and asked me to wear them.

'Look again, but this time, with these glasses, David. You will see that these people are not what they are portraying to be.'

As I put on the glasses, the whole city changed image. The city appeared to be civil and clean, with new high-rise developments replacing the old and ruined city. But there was something very scary. The city, instead of being populated with humans, now had tall, large creatures, made of a purple snail-like slimy substance walking all over the city.

I immediately took off the glasses and looked again at the people. Everything seemed to be back to normal and nothing like what I had seen through the glasses.

I then looked at Rasirine and asked her, 'What is this, Ras? What are you trying to tell me? What are these glasses made of? Who are the monstrous creatures in the glasses?'

'These are not your people, David. They are disguised monsters. Did you not see them through the cosmic ray glasses?'

'Yes, I did, but I do not understand. How can these glasses change the whole city's image and turn my people into monsters?'

'Oh, David, the cosmic ray glasses do not change the image of the city. They have the ability to penetrate through your kind of people and many other living creatures and show you exactly what their true nature is. Do you know that your city is full of other creatures living amongst your people?'

Rasirine felt my panic and said, 'Look, do you see that man sitting across from us at the table near the door?'

'Yes, I do, Ras. What about him now?'

'He is not a real human. He has disguised himself from another planet that is five thousand lightyears away from planet Earth. He is living on human flesh. He is gauging to see who from your people is going to be his next victim.'

I put back on the black ray cosmic glasses, and I looked at the man sitting near the door. He immediately turned into a purple snail-like creature gliding over the table and, in a slow pace, approached us. I instantly took off the glasses and saw the same man standing near us, looking at Rasirine. Rasirine held my hand and gave me the look.

The stranger said in a non-threatening tone of voice, 'Ah! You have an old friend of mine in your company I see, sir!'

I asked with confidence, 'Do I know you, sir?'

'Probably you do not know me, but Rasirine does!'

'Rasirine, dear, how many lightyears has it been since our last encounter, perhaps forty, fifty lightyears?'

'What is it that you want from the Neekans? Why have you come to planet Earth? Are you in search of our book too?'

'Dear Rasirine', the stranger addressed her with an air of sarcasm. 'Do not tell me that you and your people are still stuck with the idea in your mind that there is a book called *The secrets of Orchadia*? Let me tell you that there is no such book buried under the sands of planet Earth. It was all play stories and myths that your stupid, lying race sold to us too!'

'How dare you insult my people in such manner?'

'Listen, Rasirine, your race told us that there was hope that the universe could be saved. You have lured us to make this journey to planet Earth in order to assist you finding a book that has never existed.'

In a perplexed look, I faced Rasirine, expecting her to answer back to the stranger. She said nothing. Instead, she took a large breath, and within two seconds, she stood up and looked the creature straight in the eyes. Then she targeted her electronic crossbow at the stranger's heart, and her voice boomed out of her chest.

'We neekans have been enslaved, tortured, and killed on this journey just as much as your race has, and i will not allow you any further to insult my race!'

The rage in Rasirine's eyes brought a fear that bolted through me. The creature was clearly frightened by the crossbow's proximity to his vital human-like organ. He simply looked down fearfully and backed away slowly.

'I believe you, Rasirine, and I can feel the pain and suffering you are enduring. I know that the Neekans have truly been hurt in the century-long process of finding *The Secrets of Orchadia*. You and I must find the place where the book may be, for it certainly lies not in the stranger's possession.'

Rasirine agreed. 'I understand that he does not have the book. Otherwise, he would have used its secrets against the Neekans. The stranger's name is Thorkalzor.'

We left the eatery by walking out in short-paced steps whilst watching closely what Thorkalzor's next move was going to be. Rasirine had warned me that it was not the end with Thorkalzor.

Rasirine was right. As we were walking away from the eatery, approximately fifty metres away, Thorkalzor transformed himself into the purple creature I had observed through the cosmic ray glasses, but this time multiplied himself in numbers around us. Rasirine, with the speed of the light, grabbed her laser beam and pointed it towards Thorkalzor. She instructed me to do so too.

I had positioned myself in such a way that my back was against the wall and I was keeping control of Thorkalzor's multiples.

'Now!' I yelled, and Rasirine threw me a grenade.

I unscrewed the top and threw it over near to the segregated group of the creatures. The explosion created a firework display of purple skin layers and liquid fats. However, one was approaching us very quickly, and as it gained speed, I beamed it in the gut. I watched its purple blood ooze out of its skin, and the liquid soon covered the ground.

I turned around and saw another creature holding tight Rasirine's throat, restricting her breathing.

'Leave her alone!' I yelled and shot it in the arm.

It made a large roar of pain and, as it was collapsing to the ground, released Rasirine.

'Watch out!' Rasirine called.

A long silver blade from another beast sliced through the skin on my arm, and blood stained my shirt.

Rasirine shot the monstrous creature with her crossbow. The howls of pain from the dying creatures echoed through the city. Rasirine and I were standing alone and ready to fight more creatures. As we noticed no more fighters were advancing, we took a deep breath, and out of nowhere, the booming voice of Thorkalzor threatened us.

'Do not move! Stand still! I have something to say to both of you.'

'What is it now?' Rasirine asked.

'Well, Rasirine, I trust you know that this is not the end of your battle.'

'We are ready for you, Thorkalzor', I said in disdain.

'I would recommend that both of you wipe that look off your face. I have so much more fun to give you.'

'I cannot wait . . . bring it on', I responded.

'I have better soldiers with better weapons waiting for you. Laser rays and all! My laser beams are faster than your beams, Rasirine! You want a Turquoise War? You will have a Turquoise War. I am sorry for disappointing both of you, but I hope you will at least enjoy dying heroically.'

Thorkalzor left the town, turning into purple burning flames.

'How do Thorkalzor's creatures reproduce so quickly, Rasirine?'

'Every time one is born, twenty more are created out of the same cells. Take Thorkalzor's threat and warning seriously.'

'Well then!' I said. 'Let's get on with our killing!'

Rasirine gave me a disapproving look. 'David, we have to be very fast and extremely flexible in order to fight Thorkalzor's soldiers. Do you understand?'

Before I was able to respond, Rasirine, without turning her head, directed her arm in a half circle and, with her laser beam gun, shot the creature that was two metres away from us.

'How did you that!?'

'I am a woman!' She cut me off, and she shot another creature right behind me.

I charged towards the group of oncoming creatures as they primed their weapons, and I shot them repetitively with my laser beams.

'There you are, you horrific, ugly, monstrous creatures!'

The smell of burning flesh flooded the area. The creatures were multiplying even more, and they were fiercer as Thorkalzor promised us.

'Rasirine, watch out! They have a holo-gun aiming at you!' I tried to warn her.

I knew no excellent maneuvering skills would protect her from the impact of the lasers. She would instantly die. The world froze as I ran towards her. I saw the lasers leave the barrel of the gun, gliding and slicing through the air in perfect motion.

'Rasirine!' I called out with all my might and, with the speed of light, grabbed her and dragged her to the floor. I was not at a fast-enough speed. The lasers ricocheted of her shoulder and hit the back of her head.

Rasirine's turquoise flesh was singeing, and the shriek of pain was too much for me to bear. I picked her up and cradled her in my arms. She was unconscious. I was holding the gun unstably in my hand, and I aimed at the ever-approaching attackers.

'What do you want?' I cried in consternation. 'What do you want?' I yelled out to them for the second time in anger.

The creatures advanced towards me at a slower pace as they were coming closer to Rasirine and me.

Thorkalzor's voice sounded in a vibrating echo. 'Stop! This ends here and now!'

The creatures disappeared all at once. Rasirine was regaining strength as I was holding her. I looked around, but I could not see Thorkalzor anywhere. I was wondering where the voice came from.

'This little game you came here to play is quite silly', Thorkalzor's voice continued. 'Why did you come to the main city, Rasirine? And why did you bring this man here to fight with you for the book?'

Rasirine did not respond to Thorkalzor's interrogation.

'The book *The Secrets of Orchadia* does not exist. Orchadia is not the most important planet, Rasirine, and neither is Earth.'

Rasirine was using her powers to fully heal, so she refrained from providing Thorkalzor with any information.

Thorkalzor insisted, 'Why do you have this man with, Rasirine?'

'Because I love him!' was Rasirine's sharp response.

'Excuse me?' he responded.

'Yes, because we love each other, Thorkalzor.'

'What is this? You love each other?'

'Thorkalzor, you will never learn to love, and I truly pity you! You are so deluded and engrossed in your own importance that you cannot share the most beautiful feeling of love. Love is stronger than hatred, Thorkalzor!'

'Aha! Are you trying to teach me, young man?'

'Well, somebody has to do it, Thorkalzor. If you are so strong and powerful, appear before our sight like a real man! But you are not a real man, this is why you are hiding and you are just projecting your voice to intimidate us.'

'Hold your tongue, young man.'

'You are a coward, Thorkalzor! You hide away like the weakling that you are.'

'Is that so?' he answered. 'A human boy finds love in an alien turquoise-skinned girl?' he continued.

'Rasirine is not an alien! She has feelings like the humans! So what if she has turquoise skin?'

'Are you blinded, human boy? Is that why she has endangered your life? She only wants your assistance to get the supposedly book to save her planet! You were nearly going to lose your life for her.'

'It is my fault. Rasirine has done nothing to hurt me.' I stopped for a moment and looked at Rasirine. 'And I know that she never will.'

'Aha! So sweet . . . ' a sarcastic voice echoed. 'Do you want a medal, son?' he continued.

'A medal for what, Thorkalzor?' I replied furiously.

'A medal for loving my archenemy . . .'

'Leave him alone! You sound like a mangy dog that is foolishly concealed!' Rasirine howled in livid tears rushing down her face.

'Rasirine, it is all right. It does not matter what he thinks. All that matters is that I love you.' And I held her by the wrist, preventing her from doing anything irrational.

'Let's leave. It is not worth it.' I tried to put that sentence into a more positive tone of voice. I contemplated adding a faint smile to cheer off the annoyance clearly evident on Rasirine's jewel-like face.

She took a faint breath and lowered her shoulders and said, 'I suppose so'.

CHAPTER 15

As we turned to run from the city, a burning grenade fell through the sky and struck Rasirine. She fell to the ground, bleeding heavily. I heard a faint wail then complete silence that chilled me to the bone.

'No!' I cried and ran towards Rasirine's body.

'I told you!' a strange voice bellowed.

More and more grenades fell around us. I did not have much time. I picked up Rasirine's unconscious body and held her in my arms. Then I activated the body control system to run.

Rasirine's body was moving aimlessly like a ragdoll whilst I was running, holding her in my embrace. Then Thorkalzor's evil laugh came back, echoing for miles, as I was cutting through the roads of the city, holding Rasirine in my arms. The grenades seemed to stop.

I placed Rasirine's body as gently as I could on the ground and looked at her face. I could not contain myself from whispering in mixed feeling of fright and hope. 'Wake up, Ras, please, please, Rasirine. My gorgeous Rasirine, wake up.'

I stared at her face again with the hope that she might make some movement, indicating that she could hear me. However, Rasirine was silently rested and did not move.

I got up and looked around with my intense, searching human eyes, investigating every building in order to find a better and safer place to hide for the next few hours before Rasirine can employ her powers to regenerate in her healed Neekan version.

Before I was able to locate a safer hideaway, I heard Rasirine's voice calling me, 'David, David, where are we?'

I squatted down onto the soft grassy earth and said, 'Do not be preoccupied, Ras, we are safe for the time being. Do you think you can heal yourself in the next few seconds? We need to leave this area immediately.'

Rasirine felt the back of her head and, when she saw blood dripping on her fingers, looked up at me and instantaneously healed her wound.

'Thank you for saving me, David, but you could have been hurt. You should have left me there. What would have happened if you—'

I cut her off. 'That would never happen, Ras. You hear me?' She attempted to prevent me from continuing on with my next response, but she did not succeed because I said, 'I do not want to hear it, Ras! Now get up. We have got to get as far away from this city as possible!'

Rasirine jumped off the floor like a spring and was well and fit again as if she had never been injured. She hit the ground with such a fast walking pace that had me running instead of walking.

'Through the main road, David. This will take us to the highway and then to the bushes where we can rest for the night!' Rasirine commanded in an authoritative manner. Her air of confidence and conviction made me feel secure despite the fact that the sky was unnaturally calm.

'Look at the blue light, David!'

'What is it, Rasirine?'

'We must get away from it. We do not have time for me to explain it to you! Just run and keep running until we get to the bush!'

'Whatever you say, Commander in charge!' I said as I increased my running speed as much as I could. We ran and ran for so long until we finally reached the bushes. There was a strong smell of burnt wood distressing our sense of smell. Rasirine stopped for a moment and gazed around.

'What is it, Rasirine?' I asked.

'We are going to be engulfed by the flames, David. These flames are spreading through the bushes and grass plains at incredible speed.'

'Leave the spare clothes, Ras, and the tent and everything else. Just keep the laser beam guns. We must run quickly, Ras, or we will die here, and this is not how I want it to end. We need to get to our flightmobile as soon as possible, so run!'

From the distance, we could see the flightmobile parked near the tall trees near a small shed, but its entrance was blocked by the fire flames.

We stopped at a safe distance from the flames.

'Stay still, Ras, I will get you soon . . . ' And I ran through the flames to get to the flightmobile.

I smashed the window and lodged a red laser beam into the ignition for the computer to start driving it at high speed. I increased the speed to high by voice-activating the speedometer and cut through the flames.

My leg was hurting me from some injuries I had sustained, and this prevented me from maintaining a proper stand against gravity. I managed though to reach Rasirine.

'Ahhh!' she yelled. 'David . . . I do not think I—'

'Leave it and jump in! Let's go!'

Rasirine jumped in, and her body was instantly secured by the activation of a magnetic belt securing her tight on the seat. I drove the flightmobile furiously around through the miles and miles of plains. Bits of grass and rocks flew in via the broken window, making the driving even more challenging.

'Hold on, Ras!'

I screeched the vehicle forwards, and an unpleasant odour of the burning rubber entered the vehicle as I was directing it fiercely through the bushes and out to the highway.

Rasirine's hair was blown all over her face by the strong wind.

I called out to her, 'Call Glaron and Kirlan to get the others ready for the Turquoise War! This is it, Rasirine!'

Rasirine got the holo-screen and texted the message on contactogram to Glaron and Kirlan whilst I was stepping on the light speed vigorously and then suddenly on the breaks, which caused us to smash through the windscreen into the air and then dropping flat on the rocky ground.

CHAPTER 16

'Ouch!' I heard Rasirine grumble as she stood up. 'Where are we, David?'

My body had fallen with a loud thud onto the ground. 'What do you mean where are we!? You are the one who put the coordinates in the system. I was only managing the vehicle!'

She was clearly offended and, in defense, said, 'Oh yeah? Well, you are the one who was speeding like a maniac through the bushes.'

'I was only trying to save us!' I responded angrily.

'Who do you think you are? Superman, saving the world? YOLO!'

'What?' I chuckled. 'You . . . you said—'

She cut me off. 'Yes, I said YOLO. I told you that I have been studying your culture for many years. You did not expect that, did you?'

'What does it mean? Come on, tell me', I said in an inquisitive manner.

'It means "you only live once" in your language.'

'Bravo! You are a champion!'

I could not stay mad at Rasirine for long. She had this special way of conversing in human language, which made her even more adorable.

'Back to work, Ras, check the coordinates. What do they read? Are we still in England?'

She gave a weak sigh and said, 'About that, David . . . ' Then she corrected, 'No, I do not think we are on Earth anymore.'

'Not on Earth? How could we not be on Earth? The craft was specifically calibrated for travelling just on planet Earth!'

'Do you think that someone has altered the readings?'

'No, no one could have changed them', I replied, infuriated.

'Shhh! I think I heard faint footsteps in the distance.'

'Rasirine, did you hear that?' I stopped talking, and the footsteps were getting louder and louder. 'Did you hear the footsteps, Ras?'

'What footsteps, David? I think the sudden and harsh fall to the ground has affected your hearing.'

'Shhh!' I whispered, placing my finger to my lips.

After a few seconds, Rasirine heard the footsteps too. Her face immediately changed from being calm to being concerned.

'This way!' Rasirine said and pointed north.

After a lengthy run, I was exhausted and asked Rasirine, 'Where are we going, Ras, to planet Mars?'

'No, David, do you know what it is like on Mars?'

'Of course I know! Humans have been travelling to Mars from the beginning of this millennium.'

Rasirine found a secret passage, which we cautiously entered in, and sat down to regain our breath.

'There you are, David. Now you can tell me all about your knowledge of Mars.'

'Well, Mars is red and rough. It has a rocky red soil because of the iron oxide that exists on its surface.'

Rasirine was impressed by my knowledge on a planet that I have never set foot on.

'OK, David, I will tell you something about Mars that you probably do not know.'

'I am listening, Ras, shoot.'

'Mars has the largest volcano in your solar system. The height of the volcano is twenty-two kilometres. It is approximately three times higher than your tallest mountain on your planet Earth. I think its name is Mount Everest, right?'

Then something strange happened to Rasirine. She was not looking at me in the eye anymore.

I approached her and asked, 'Where did you drop the flare? We need it as it is too dark in this secret passage.'

She turned around and looked at me. She stood still and said in a commanding voice, 'I am not Rasirine.'

Her voice had changed. 'We are the Kaxonites. You are a human. Prepare to be taken to your hostage area.'

Large metal clasps held me. I was immobilised by fear. I did not know how to react or what to say, but I shouted, 'What!? No! Get off me!'

I squirmed from the Kaxonite's embrace and attempted to wiggle my body, but I was tired and exhausted from the long run. I fought as much as my human strength and power allowed me. As a result of my injuries and the weight of the clasps, I felt my body collapsing, and in an instant, I fell asleep.

CHAPTER 17

I woke up with a metal frame around my body. I tried to worm myself out, but I could not. The room was dark, and large lights were pointing straight into my eyes.

'Where am I? Can someone tell me?' I tried to lift my arm to grab the frame. Some wires were attached to my body.

'What are these wires for?'

Nobody answered my questions, but a deep voice said, 'Human, do not be disturbed. We have hooked you up to our machines.'

I looked across the triangular-shaped room, and I observed a strange-looking machine spitting out pages and pages with symbols on them that I could not decipher.

In a blink of an eye, I saw again the creature that had enslaved me. I did not know how long I had been here for, but what I had noticed was that my injuries were healed. Not a single scar remained on my body. I looked around to see if Rasirine was somewhere there in the background.

'Rasirine, are you here?' I called out.

There was no response. I started getting very anxious and frightened again. I commenced breathing heavily to the point where I was on the verge of crying. I was lost. Everything seemed to be futile. My compelling journey to save the universe came to a halt before it even started! I had failed.

'Human, we know exactly what you are thinking', the deep voice spoke.

'Who are you? Why have you captured me? I am no use to you. I only wanted to save the Neekans' planet, Orchadia, from burning and to prevent the destruction of the whole universe.'

I tried to push myself out again, and my body smacked against the casing.

'David!' a weak voice sounded. 'David, is that you?' I immediately recognised the voice. It was Rasirine's.

'Rasirine? Come closer to the frame if it is you.'

The sound of her voice brought the urge to escape back into my mind. I had to get out. I had promised to care for her, and I would not allow my words to vanish with nothing to show for it.

'We are not safe, David', Rasirine's voice warned me.

Then a huge flame lit the triangular room, and for a moment, I saw Rasirine falling on the ground. Her face was tilted to the side, and her eyes were completely shut.

Rasirine's face did not have eyebrows marking her eyes; neither had she any eyelashes on her eyelids. It reminded me of the famous painting of Mona Lisa.

'That's a good girl! Now, sleep!' a rough and evil voice called out from the shadows.

'As for you, boy, do you really think you will be able to escape?' I did not answer his question immediately, but instead, I breathed heavily and prepared for the pain that was about to surely come.

Then I replied, 'Yes, I do.'

I heard the footsteps walk slowly towards me.

The voice became angrier and more determined to punish me for my insolence. 'You are wrong!' And he turned on the electricity.

I screamed like the howler monkey whose deep growls can travel up to four kilometres, if not more, as the volts were flowing through my veins, sending pain throughout my body and to every single cell.

Just for an instance, I lost all consciousness. The lights turned off, and it felt like I was back asleep. I did not open my eyes. I wanted them to think that I was in a deep sleep. I remained lying on the floor in my casing, silent and unmoving.

'That will take care of them for now', I heard another voice say.

'How long do you propose to keep them here?' a softer female voice echoed through the room.

'We cannot keep them here forever. You know of the duty they must do!'

'I totally agree and let's say if it is not for their race, it will be beneficial then for ours!'

'That is true, Sulonia. Our race must be preserved at any cost, and in order to achieve this, we need the boy.'

'And the Neekan girl . . . ', Sulonia interjected.

'You heard what the prophets of Orchadia had said. Without his love for Rasirine, he shall not fight and win. He will lose his spirit. He shall bring upon the universe a gift so very kind. He shall save each one of us for he has everyone in mind. Do not attempt to stop him for he will find his way. Give him trouble, give him pain, but he will not be defeated.'

The other creature sighed.

'Oh, my dear child, these are fables. They are not true! A mere boy with hardly any intelligence cannot save the universe!'

The lights were lowered, and both creatures walked out of the room.

I had noticed in my silent moments of listening that their defenses were lowered as they did not fear the sleeping. I disconnected all the wires from my body and stealthily managed to climb out of my casing and went over to Rasirine, who was still lying on the floor.

'Psst, Ras! Wake up!' And I touched her face to feel if she was warm.

She stirred uneasily and tried to lift her head and faintly asked, 'What, where?'

I stopped her from speaking by placing my palm on her mouth. 'Shh! We need to get our guns back first. Have you completely healed?'

'Yes, I am fine, David. Search for our guns. We do not have time. We need to save the universe.'

'We will, Rasirine. Just be a little bit more patient.' I got up and searched the room for our laser beam guns. I found them behind the machine, hidden in a metallic drawer.

I gave Rasirine her gun, and before our exit from the laboratory, I pelted bullets at every computer and machine in the room. Mugs, holo-pads, tables, and seats overturned and were pierced with bullet holes.

'Do you like the redecoration?' I sarcastically asked Rasirine.

The laser beams and the noise from the overturning objects alarmed the creatures, and they run to see what had happened.

As soon as they opened the door and witnessed the havoc in the room, I asked them, 'Would you like us to do the same to you?'

The creatures whimpered and tried to hide behind a cabinet beside the door.

I knew that they could hear me, so I said, 'Know this, Kaxonites, when David makes a promise. He keeps it. I will not kill you for I pity your stupidity. Let us go, and in return, I will save your race too.'

The creatures retreated from their cabinet and slowly came towards us. They said nothing but opened the doors and plotted coordinates onto their transporter. We stood in the light and waited.

The feeling of teleporting came upon us again. The creatures had regretted setting us free, and I sensed that they too were afraid if the universe was going to be destroyed. However, they closed the portal.

Instantly, we were back on planet Earth in search of *The Secrets of Orchadia* book.

The city was in a chaotic state since our departure. Armed policemen and soldiers were ready to attack and defend the city and its civilians.

CHAPTER 18

I pressed the teleport button to transport Rasirine and myself. I felt the air shifting around my body, and I heard Rasirine asking, 'Where are we going!?'

I covered her eyes and replied, 'We are going to paradise!'

'Really?' Then she pointed at the disheveled city of London. 'Actually, I have fallen in love with London. I really like this city', Rasirine remarked. 'David, did you manage to communicate with Glaron and Kirlan?'

'No, I have not been able to get in touch with Kirlan, but I have sent a message to Glaron on contactogram. Check if he has replied, Ras.'

My thigh had a deep cut and was giving me a bit of trouble standing up straight. Rasirine saw it and straight away employed her healing powers to bring the wounded flesh back to normal. I was impressed by the advanced skills the Neekans had to heal and recuperate any kind of flesh.

Rasirine checked on the contactogram and saw that Glaron had left us a short note.

'Glaron has responded!'

'Right now, read his note aloud please!'

Rasirine read out loud the message as I sat next to her.

Do not worry, they are all dead. By the time you get here this place should be a ghost town. We are stopping for now. I have organized everyone to meet back here.

Just a short reminder: 'Individual attacks are not working well and not on a major scale anyway as it was anticipated'.

We have been hearing about your triumphs. Keep up the good work.

Glaron

After reading Glaron's message, Rasirine said, 'Do you want to head for the mountains? That is where paradise is for me'.

'Why not?' and I keyed in to the teleport the directions for the mountains.

'I feel like hiking through the foothills of your tall mountains. I want to see your rainforests. They are very important for your planet because they help your people breathe by absorbing the carbon dioxide, and in return, they release oxygen, which humans need.'

'Yes, precisely, Ras, our rainforests are the lungs of our planet.'

'Then why did your people destroy vast areas of them?'

'They did not realise the value of them until the end of the last millennium.'

'The Neekans always referred to them as your "rainforest pharmacy", and we have developed further from your ways.'

'How did the Neekans use our rainforest plants for medicinal purposes?'

'The Neekans did not take any of your rainforest plants because we do not have the diseases that you humans have.'

'I do not understand, Ras. What are you saying? You are confusing me.'

'For example, David, when you get a cut, we have powers to heal any flesh wound, which you humans do not yet have.'

'And how is that relevant to the rainforests?'

'Listen, for example, leukemia does not exist in Orchadia.'

'Anyway your skin has turquoise colour. Even if you had leukemia, nobody would be able to tell. Do Neekans ever get a pale yellow skin colour?'

'David, leukemia has nothing to do with the colour of the skin. It is the humans' red blood cells that become deficient. The "rosy periwinkle" plant found in Madagascar is a plant that you humans use for the cure of leukemia.'

'Are you a doctor, Ras?'

'No, I am a princess, David, and my duty is to protect my people. I have to be well informed about diseases and other things too.'

'Yes, I understand, but how come you know so much about humans?'

'I have studied your planet for many years.'

'What else do you know?'

'You humans have learnt only one per cent of how to use these amazing plants that exist in the rainforest. So imagine the possibilities if you could experiment with the other ninety-nine per cent.'

We came across a large body of water after four hours of walking. I did not mind because I was learning a lot from Rasirine.

'Ras, I am very impressed with the things you are telling me, and I would like to ask you, do you really want to continue being a part of this war, or is your main purpose to find the book?'

'I am here searching for the book, David, but if your people fight us because they think we are invaders, we have to engage in war with the humans.'

'I know, Rasirine. Why do you think I have joined forces with you?'

'We need to cross this lake, David.'

'You can even swim, Ras?'

'Yes, David, and without thinking that I am praising myself, I think that I am an even better swimmer than you.'

We swam for a few metres across the lake, and when we got to about halfway, I felt something constantly brushing up against my foot. For a moment I thought it was Ras playing games with me, and I shouted to her, 'Stop trying to kick me, Ras!'

'I am not kicking you! What are you trying to say?' she replied annoyed.

Then I felt it again. This time, I started to panic, and flashes of imaginary malicious creatures entered my perception. And I said to Rasirine, 'I swear it is not funny, Ras!'

'I am not doing anything—' And she suddenly uttered a cry, 'Ahhhh!' as she was dragged into the water below.

'Rasirine!' I called in desperation.

The last of her blue hair was seen just under the surface of the water. I froze with fear. I did not know what to do.

I tried swimming underneath the water, but something kept me above the surface as if it did not want me to see where my Rasirine was taken.

I took a deep breath and dove straight down into the water. I tried to open my eyes under the now-green murky water to gauge my surroundings, but there was no sign of Rasirine anywhere. Whatever malicious creature had taken her really wanted to make sure that she could not be found.

My lungs were exhausted and longed for a breath of air. I forced my body farther down in the water before I rose to the surface to get some air. My eyes bulged with the pressure of the murky water, and my eardrums were beating hard against my brain.

Just as I was about to rush back up to the surface for air, I noticed a face. It was staring at me with a menacing look. I was alarmed and mortified at the same time. I swam with incredible speed from the bottom of the lake to the surface.

I broke through the surface and hastily took a large breath. Before I was able to take a second breath, I thought I was having double vision and seeing things. I saw a large green hand extending towards my body in an attempt to catch me.

I tried to swim away from it, but it grabbed my legs and pulled me straight down through the water. Water was filling my nostrils, and my vision was blurred. I tried to swim back up, but I could not.

CHAPTER 19

I woke up in a glass building deep underneath the lake. I could see the same murky green water through the glass house. I was locked in a golden barred cage this time, with gems decorating both the inside and the outside.

At the main entrance of the glass house, I noticed a label hanging on the handle of the glass door, 'The One Who Will Save the Universe'. *Is that what the various civilizations from the surrounding galaxies spread across the universe about me?* I wondered for a moment.

I was feeling very sore, and my legs could not hold me up; however, I forgot all about my pain and felt pride and joy rising in me. I was proud of myself especially when I read the sign written in proper letters of the alphabet instead of funny symbols.

'Not at all pompous are we, Mr. Saviour?' I heard Rasirine's voice uttering the half-question and half-sarcasm phrase. She continued, 'What is your name, lad?'

'Me, saviour? What are you talking about, Ras?'

'Do not call me Ras. My name is Rasirine.'

'Well, and I am some stupid kid from inner London whom you, Rasirine, chose to name as "the savior of the universe". Do you remember me promising you to save your planet from burning into ashes?'

'Of course, I do remember, young lad.'

'Then why do you ask for my name?'

'I just want to make sure that it is you, the real "savior" of my planet.'

'Then, Rasirine, what type of games are you playing with me? Am I seeing or thinking all these events, or are they real? Are you my Rasirine?'

'I am Rasirine. You bumped into me when I was swimming in the lake.'

'Well, shame on you, Mrs. Rasirine, for swimming a little too close to me.'

'You are extremely handsome, young man', she said in a seductive manner.

I realised then that this woman was not Rasirine even though she sounded and looked like my Rasirine.

Instead of getting all mad about her untruthfulness and her inconsistencies, I decided to continue with her game.

'I know my good looks are incredibly hard to handle, but you will just have to learn for next time, young lady, to stay away from good-looking strangers?'

She was sitting quite comfortably across me, and when she heard my comment, she put a playful little grin across her face and responded, 'Don't I now? Well, perhaps we should meet again and see who really came much too close for comfort?'

'So you say it was uncomfortable Ra—' I was about to say her nickname but refrained from doing so, and instead I said, 'Rasi . . . whatever your name is.'

'Yes, it really was. But I did not mind. You are quite a handsome young man.'

There was a hissing-like noise, and a tall and extremely pale woman appeared.

'Am I interrupting you, Rasirine?' she asked in a quite disturbed manner.

I lifted my head, and I looked at the woman. *I have seen this woman before*, I thought to myself. But where I could not remember. She looked so strikingly familiar that I was certain I had met her once again in the past but could not pinpoint where and how exactly we got to meet.

The woman turned and asked me sternly, 'Tell me, young man, what you are here for? There are no people lining this part of England. Why are you here?'

I fumbled through various different possibilities that ran through my head; should I say we are clowns or maybe we are spies? Oh no, definitely not spies because we would get shot for that. I looked again at the woman, and her harsh eyes pierce through my eyes.

I responded, 'We are two retired soldiers who wish to have a break from any war taking place. We want to have a rest'.

Initially, it seemed like a good answer, but it did not impress, neither convinced, the strange woman.

'I see!' she responded with evident unhappiness.

'Do retired soldiers carry their weapons with them wherever they go?'

'No, no, madam, we carry those weapons for our own protection. We are looking for a place to escape from the war that has just begun. The Turquoise War, you may have heard?'

'I do not appreciate such unpleasantries, young man. Are you intending to give me an honest answer?'

'Madam, we found those laser beam guns in the city. We thought that they would be useful to defend ourselves from unwelcome attackers. In addition, do you not think it is quite silly to leave stray weapons lying around unattended?'

'Which city are you referring to?'

'The city of London, madam.'

'You have destroyed the city? You have ripped it apart? There are dead bodies lying everywhere. Do not tell me that I have to believe that the dead bodies would make use of the laser beam guns?'

'No, I am not asking you to believe that at all, madam. Quite the contrary, you could have used those guns inappropriately', I told her boldly.

'What?' she said, more of a statement of anxiety than one of question.

'Oh please, madam! For your information, I am the boy who will save the universe.'

'Really?' she responded, half smirking.

'Do you think I have been given this task because I have not any intelligence?' She was about to say something, but I interrupted her, 'You never thought I would recognise your robotic mermaids, did you?'

'Have we met before, boy?'

'Perhaps. Who knows?'

'How do you know about my robotic mermaids?'

I did not want to answer her question, and instead, I attacked her with another statement. 'By the way, madam, really, get your robotic mermaids fixed. They are confusing beams with magnetic waves.'

The woman was clearly very offended at my rude remark and responded with annoyance, 'I will not have you in my underworld palace of Tectonia uttering disrespectful comments about my mermaids. Thank you!'

I had caught her out. I knew where we were now. I pretended to be surprised.

'You what? Who has a palace underneath the waters?'

Her lips tightened even more and, in her anger, accidentally pressed a button on the remote control, allowing the bars of the cages to collapse and for her to vanish. Rasirine ran toward me and whispered something in my ear as I was about to run too.

Rasirine pulled me back. Without a single word, she pointed towards the glass wall, which was keeping the building safe under the murky water.

'Look up, David', she fearfully whispered.

I raised my eyes to the top of the wall. There were bodies floating. They were coming out of an outlet into the lake's green murky water. The lifeless bodies glided through the water and soon they became food for the carnivorous fish.

All of a sudden, I felt a strange little poke on the side of my leg and a little girl's voice calling out to us, 'Good way to leave, is it not?'

Rasirine and I turned around to face her. She stood there body covered in measles and eyes red and inflamed, her mouth frothing, a large silver growth on the left side of her face.

'Do not worry, they are not dead. I was told by the high priestess that they are just going for a visit. I will be going too . . . today actually.'

Rasirine and I exchanged frightened looks.

'What do you mean "they're just going for a visit", sweetie?' I asked in great curiosity.

The girl looked puzzled.

'You have not been here long, have you?'

We shook our heads to signal a no.

'When you are really sick, you go to the sanctuary through that shark over there. He does not devour you. He transports you to the healers.'

This did not make any sense, and the girl noticed that we were very confused.

'Do not worry. You are not sick like me, so you won't go through the pipes. You will die here instead', she said smiling and then skipped off towards a dark corridor.

From the same dark corridor, the strange woman reappeared. 'I see you have met my daughter', she said in a voice filled with sadness.

'How old is your daughter, madam, if I may ask?'

'She is almost thirty years old in human years, but she is very sick.'

'What is wrong with her?'

'In your human race, you call this "mental illness". I do not know what the Neekans call this illness.'

Rasirine approached her and tried to sympathise with her. 'Madam, we do not have those illnesses in Orchadia and many other illness that exist on planet Earth, so we do not have a specific name for, it but we adopt the name that you label your illnesses with.'

'Will your daughter be all right?' I asked her with concern.

Tears started filling her eyes and flowing down her face.

'No, she will never be normal again', she said and continued crying.

Rasirine put her arm around the woman and sat her down on the stool.

'Madam, putting aside all the ideas and perceptions you have of us, please know that we feel so sorry for losing your child and that we understand the pain you are going through. We will do whatever it takes to help you and your daughter', Rasirine told her with a most caring voice.

The woman looked back to us and said, 'I have misjudged you both. Unfortunately, there is nothing that can be done to save my daughter. She is ill beyond help'. And she buried her face in her hands.

'It was my fault! My fault all along!' she was saying, angrily blaming herself.

I put my hands on the woman's shoulders and shook her slightly to divert her attention towards me. 'Look straight into my eyes', I gently ordered her.

The woman shook her head in despair and refused to look at me.

'Look at me', I insisted for the second time.

The woman raised her head and looked at me with an expression full of guilt and sadness.

'Listen to me well and good. I might be human, but most humans have a lot of compassion for all creatures. It is not your fault. You must believe me on this', I said trying to convince her otherwise. I could not stand seeing others suffering whether they were dear to me or just strangers.

'Boy, you do not understand. I brought my daughter here to teach her the robotics! I thought the palace of Tectonia would be a safe place for her! However, I was proven wrong. Instead, she became delusional.'

Rasirine held the woman's feeble hand and, with conviction, replied to the woman, 'Your daughter will develop into a new individual when she gets older. Please have faith in the Neekans' prophecies.'

'How do you know, dear?' the woman said as she was regaining hope.

'I am a Neekan, madam, and you knew this information from the time you captured me and have kept me captive in the palace of Tectonia with my human friend. You are from the race of the Levistems, are you not, madam?'

The woman gasped and, with a large smile on her face, said, 'You knew I was a Levistem?'

'Of course, madam, and I am aware that your people have been kind to the Neekans, and I will help your daughter survive the change. I promise.'

The woman's face lit like sunlight, and her face expressed hope.

'I will bring Starlenia back here so you can heal her. You stay here.'

The woman vanished back into the darkness.

'What is happening, Ras? Is the girl going to be okay?' Rasirine gave me an honest look.

'The girl will be fine. The only hurdle to overcome is that she is half Levistem and half human. The change is too great for her human body to tolerate. She may not be able to pull through. It is a very difficult procedure, and the healing process is quite severe.'

'Honestly, Rasirine, do not be scared. I believe in your Neekan powers, and you will save the girl.'

The woman came back from the dark corridor, bringing her daughter on to a bed that was equipped with every possible surgical tool a surgeon could ask for.

'Please hurry!' the woman asked.

'I will, but you must leave now. I need my space for the procedure to go well.'

She took out the scalpel and made an incision through the little girl's arm. Blood from the artery squirted everywhere. I could not watch. I left the room and followed the woman in the dark corridor. I saw her standing a few metres away from the lit entrance of the room.

The woman put her arm on my shoulder, and the sadness of her face was immediately gone.

'Come with me, boy', the woman asked me to follow her.

I did not want to follow her because I was thinking of Rasirine and the healing process of the girl. The woman started peeling. Her orange skin peeled off her face first, revealing a large metal casing, but my body was weak, and paralysis had set in. The last words that I was able to hear were, 'Good night, you stupid fool!'

CHAPTER 20

'You are a liar!' I heard a scream of fury through the walls.

I could recognise that voice anywhere. I banged onto the wall behind me and called out as loud as I could have, 'Rasirine, what is wrong!'

I fell to my knees, my head sliding against the cold wall. It was dark. Darkness you would never believe. Pitch-black like as if my eyes had been blinded.

'Oh! Poor little David is afraid, is he not? Do not worry. Rasirine won't die easy. You will be able to hear her shrieks of pain from miles!' She cackled away.

This woman honestly made me change my mind about her. She forced me to alter how I think and how I will look at her and her world from now on.

My mind was spinning with the different possibilities of what could be happening to Rasirine. I did not know where I was or the whereabouts of Rasirine. I did not know how I was going to escape.

I stood up, my head barely touching the ceiling, and felt around the room. It was small. Two steps to my left and I hit a wall. Two steps to the right, I hit a door. I shook the door handle vigorously. Nothing happened.

'Let me out!' I yelled in the darkness.

'Oh, what is that I hear? You want me to let you out?' the woman's hoarse voice asked in an unpleasant tone.

'Yes, let me go. Let Rasirine and I go! What is it that you want from us?'

Her evil voice whispered to me from all the angles of the room. 'I will make a deal then, shall I?'

I had to change my frame of thinking and the quadrants in my plans.

'You lied about your own child being sick. You were untruthful about your species. You are deceitful in your nature, and this alone makes you very ugly and not to be trusted however great you may think you are.'

'David! I can hear you', Rasirine's voice called from behind me. I ran to the wall and banged my hands on it.

'Ras!' I cried. A few tears ran down my face. 'I'm sorry, I am so, so, sorry'

'Shut up!' the woman yelled at the top of her voice.

The sound of a large metal bang behind me caused me to jump. Someone was hurting Rasirine. Her screams were repetitive and loud, churning a pain inside my stomach, which then amounted to anger.

'Let her go!' I howled. By that time, I had lost my temper, and I was becoming wild.

'My dear David, it is no use conducting yourself in that manner. Every time you speak to her, I get my servants to slice part of her leg with a metal knife with time-filled energy that sends her to the past.'

I was downright disorientated when I heard the woman describing the excruciating pain that Rasirine was put under. I did not know how long this was going to continue for and how much time have we had spent in this underworld's horrific palace.

I was here, and suddenly, memories of faraway times repossessed my thoughts. I saw myself fighting the war. I saw slaves everywhere. I felt no love permeating among people. I was lost. It felt like somebody was controlling my thinking and I had no power of it.

A spray of some kind of indistinguishable fragrance then fell upon my face. I felt very drowsy. The last words I was able to retain clearly in my mind were, 'Go to sleep, dear. The deal will continue.'

I woke up to a woman's voice calling me persistently with intensity. 'David, are you there? David, please respond. David, I need to hear that you are there.'

I could hardly utter any words. I just tapped on the wall to give a sign that I was still here, imprisoned in this small room.

I heard the woman choking on her tears. 'David, it is me, Rasirine!' She then stopped for a moment to continue on saying, 'I've been waiting two years here for you. Two years of your silence. Please tell me you remember me. Please'.

The name rang a bell. However, some kind of amnesia had taken over me, and I was not able to remember who this woman was with the name Rasirine. She kept talking to me, but still I was not able to remember her.

Then she said, 'Orchadia is going to burn to ashes, and the universe will be destroyed, David.'

All of a sudden, emotions and memories flooded my mind. How could I have forgotten my mission? How could I have forgotten the angelic voice of my sweet Rasirine that I had fallen in love with?

'Ras! Of course I remember you. Where am I? My mind has been closed off. How has it been two years that you have been waiting for me when it has only been moments before that I last heard your voice?' I was scared and unable to understand. This whole situation was confusing me with these perplexing memory accounts.

'No, David, it has been two whole years . . . ' And then she stopped.

The woman's horrible voiced echoed through the walls and straight into my ears. 'Oh, I see that you have both woken up from your hibernation.'

She then continued on to sound as if she was being the reasonable one. 'Do you both want to hear the deal or not?' She paused for a moment, waiting for our response.

'So you are both not responding . . . All right then, I will proceed with my proposal, and I suggest you listen closely since it will be your getaway to freedom. One of you must give me your soul and your memories in order for the other to survive.'

None of us made a sound. We were both horrified by her suggestion, but we had no other alternative since freedom was waiting for us in one way or another.

'I will do it!' I said. 'But you must let Rasirine go immediately!'

Rasirine interrupted me. 'No! I will do it, David! You take my soul and let David go!'

'Rasirine, what are you doing! Don't say that! I won't let you live a life of no memories and emotions!'

'Neither will I, David!' she screamed back.

The woman was not able to understand the superior emotion of love that existed between Rasirine and I, and she indifferently asked, 'Are you sure, Rasirine, darling, you will do that for this lazy young man? I mean you did wait two whole years and now you want to give up your life and soul for him?'

Rasirine and I could both see that this evil and unkind woman was trying to turn one against the other. However, Rasirine answered, 'It was not his fault'.

Before I could answer, this villain woman created a very strong pain hit my chest, and I woke up in a different state and frame of mind. My arms were feeble, and wrinkles had covered my arms and face.

'Rasirine, where are you?' I called out to see if Rasirine was able to hear me.

'What is wrong, David? I am right here! On the other side of the wall'

'It has been forty-five years. What took you so long?' I responded in a voice that was tired, old, and strained.

'David, it has not been forty five years. It has been five minutes only. What is this malicious woman doing to you?' Rasirine said indignantly.

'I am old and feeble, Rasirine. I can see how my skin has badly wrinkled.'

'It cannot be forty-five years, David. I have not changed. I look exactly the same. This cannot be true. Do not believe it. You must regain back control of your mind.'

'How can I do that, Ras? I am not a Neekan. I do not have superpowers like your race.'

'Listen to me and concentrate very hard on what I will be asking you to do. Think of this wall falling down and us reuniting!'

'OK, Rasirine. I am thinking about it.'

'David, it is not just enough to think about us being together, but you must make vivid pictures in your head of us being free and reunited. Do you understand?'

As those pictures were formed in my mind my skin returned to normal and I heard a happy cry from Rasirine next door. 'Yes, you did it, David. You did it!'

'Stop! What are doing?!' The evil woman's shriek echoed off the walls. 'You are both ruining my plan!!!'

Rasirine was no longer scared of the malicious woman and gave me further instructions, 'Think of the wall collapsing now, David!'

I did as she told me. I pictured the wall collapsing bit by bit, and I pictured the lights all turning on. I pictured the door unlocking and that all my strength had returned to me. As I thought of these things they happened. I saw Rasirine running through the collapsed door and holding me tight.

'The door!' Rasirine shrieked.

We ran to the door and pushed it open. The metallic woman was standing there, hooked up to the system with her eyes closed.

Rasirine went over to examine the metal casing. 'She was never here in the first place, David.'

'What?' I exclaimed. 'What do you mean she was never here? She was here! She locked us up in a cupboard and blackmailed us.'

'That was not her', Rasirine said.

She paused and caught her breath. 'This woman is a hologram. She died many lightyears ago, and she was only trying to protect her broken ship from intruders.'

I attempted to interrupt her, but Rasirine continued on. 'Even the girl, her sick daughter, she was a hologram too. This palace she made reference to be a fully functioning ship, but now it exists only in the memories.'

I took all this in and asked Rasirine one question, 'Does this mean . . . ?'

Rasirine answered my question before I could finish it.

'Yes, it does mean this was never real. This was all a dream. We are still swimming, David. The mermaids took our consciousness, but we can regain it through a conscious decision to wake up from the dream on the count of three. Are you ready?'

'What do I have to focus on? Tell me precisely, Ras.'

Rasirine gave me this grimace that made her look so cute with her drawn-on eyebrows on her turquoise skin and the implanted fake eyelashes on her eyelids. She did this because she wanted to resemble the humans, as she disclosed to me in confidence.

'Focus on waking up, right?'

'Ready when you are ready, Ras.'

'On three, you start!'

'One, two, three! Go!'

'That was fun!' I told Rasirine as we continued on with our swimming.

'What was fun?' she asked me blankly.

It felt like my heart had stopped beating for a moment. Had she lied to me? Was it really Rasirine? Probably she was an imposter. Who knows? Probably Rasirine had given her soul and memories away to let me live.

Incarcerated in my hypothetical thoughts, I neglected responding to the question Rasirine had asked me, so she fired another question, but this time, her tone of voice was not as enthusiastic as it appeared to be before.

'Who are you?'

My face froze with fear.

'What is wrong, David?' Rasirine asked in a more concerned manner this time.

I sighed with a deep breath of relief. 'Sorry, Ras, it took me a while to come back to our present state because I tried to remember what it was like in the underwater palace.'

'I will remind you David. It was horrible, cold, and miserable.'

'Despite that, Ras, did you see that the dark corridor was filled with photos of us? Tell me, did you notice our photos in the darkness?'

'No, I did not notice any photos. Are you sure it was not the malicious woman trying to play with your thoughts again?'

'What did you see, Ras?'

'I just saw a plain confined room'

'No, Ras, it was not just a plain room', I insisted. 'I think that woman made you colour blind for the whole time you were down there. She knew very well that the Neekans have the most exquisite colours in the whole universe.'

'David, please allow me to explain. It was your memories.'

'My memories? How? What are you saying, Ras?'

'Your memories of our past experiences together and your ardent feelings of love for me were so strong that they got imprinted on to the walls in the human form of photos.'

'Why on the wall?'

'The Levistem woman tried to take your memories away from you, but because she was not able to do so, they were instead imprinted on the wall.'

'How could she detect the energy of love? It is a human feeling transmitted through waves that cannot be detected underwater.'

'This is where you are mistaken, David. Your energy on the emotion of love is too strong, and the woman was not able to handle. If she did not ally with you, and this is why she called you to go with her in the dark corridor, the powerful energy would have destroyed her ship to smithereens.'

A tear slid down my face.

CHAPTER 21

Rasirine and I continued swimming towards the shore. As we reached the sand, Rasirine collapsed and held her stomach.

'David, I think our baby will be joining us soon.'

'You will give birth to our baby?'

I was shocked and paralysed with fear. I did not know how to respond or what to do in a situation like this.

'That is impossible, Ras!'

'I am a Neekan, David, are you forgetting it?'

'Are you sure it is not the evil woman of the ship playing tricks on our minds?'

'No, David, the evil woman has died many lightyears ago. Please go and set up the tent. I need to rest.'

I did as I was told because Ras was much smarter than me and has seen more of the universe than I will probably ever see in all my human living years.

I set up the tent and made a nice fireplace with nearby rocks and lit the fire with some sticks that I cut of from the tree branches. Then I went hunting for some fish in the lake so that I could feed Rasirine and myself.

When I got back to the tent, I saw Rasirine resting on the ground and a little girl besides her sleeping.

'You are late', she said in an exhausted voice.

'What? Where is the . . . are you? Is the little child sleeping next to you our baby?' I managed to finally ask the question.

'Yes, yes! I had her in a grown-up form. This is how the female Neekans give birth to babies in Orchadia.'

'Well, that was . . .'

'Quick? Yes, it was. I am from Orchadia. It is very simple for us.'

I was lost and excited at the same time. I did not know what to say. I was curious to see what our child looked like. I approached Rasirine quietly and asked her if I could see our little girl.

Rasirine unwrapped the towel, and the little girl's face appeared in the dim firelight. She had the human characteristics as she was sleeping peacefully. Then she opened her eyes, and two extremely big light-blue eyes sparkled as I touched her little face.

'Hello there!' I said as softly as I could in an attempt to hide my unstoppable excitement. 'You are so beautiful', I whispered.

My little girl wriggled in her mother's arms and giggled as I made funny faces to her.

'Who is the beautiful girl in this tent? You are!' And I tickled her a little bit. My little daughter giggled and batted her tiny eyelashes in protest to the tickle monster.

'Yes, she is beautiful, is she not?'

'Of course she is gorgeous! Do not forget, this is my daughter.' Rasirine laughed.

'I can see her being a Daddy's girl. You are going to spoil her. Did you notice that she looks like you?'

'Like me? No way! Look at her eyes, those are your eyes.' Rasirine blushed.

'Half human, half Neekan', I said.

'Do you think she is going to be discriminated against in the human race?' Rasirine asked me in a half-disappointed manner.

I looked at Rasirine and felt her pain. 'No, she won't because she has the two people who will save the universe as her parents.' And I paused.

'Now, let us think of more beautiful things. What will we call her!?'

'Hmmm!' Rasirine mumbled. 'I was thinking of the name Lunette. What do you think, David?'

'Lunette? Well, Rasirine, this is the most beautiful name I have ever heard. How did you come up with this name? Lunette it is our daughter's name.'

Lunette seemed to understand what her mother and I were talking about. For a moment, she gazed up at us and smiled with her adorable little dimples showing.

'Shh, go back to sleep now, Lunette. It is very late.' Lunette shut her eyes and fell back to sleep as Rasirine sung her a lullaby that almost put me to sleep.

Within a few minutes, Lunette was sleeping quietly underneath the blankets in her mother's arms. Rasirine placed her on the grass bed that she had made whilst I had gone. Then we stepped quietly outside and sat around the fire, eating the fish that was just freshly cooked.

It was getting late in the night, and we wondered about the future. Our weapons were soaking wet, and there were no animals around to hunt for our breakfast. Rasirine started singing, and she sang and sang and sang till all the mountains were covered by her sweet voice.

The stars were shining so brightly over us, but I could not stop thinking of the Neekans and their planet. I could only imagine the worry Rasirine's people were going through as the days were coming nearer to the destruction of Orchadia.

Whilst other civilizations were stuck in a state of oblivion, here we were the two most important people in this colossal universe, trying to change what has been written in the prophecies. My mind was drifting away as the song was putting all the plants and birds to sleep around us.

Lunette stayed perfectly quiet through the night, which allowed Rasirine and I to get a few hours' sleep.

When I woke up the next morning, I remembered that last night, I dreamt of wild horses running through the clouds living on Orchadia where I would be respected and hailed for the salvation of the Neekans.

I dreamt of Lunette fighting across the universe with us and saving the world as she grew into a heroine of her own.

I suddenly heard Lunette's voice greeting me, 'Good morning, Daddy!'

I was taken by surprise, 'Good morning, prinnnncess. How are you this morning?'

'I am well, Daddy, where is Mummy? I am hungry.'

'Ras, you did not tell me that out daughter could talk?' I said in bewilderment.

'I am sorry, David. We have been together for such a long time that I take it for granted that you know everything about the Neekans. I have just realised that I need to constantly tell you things about the Neekan ways.'

'One moment please, Ras. I know that your race is very advanced in comparison to humans, but to the extent of giving birth to already grown-up children who can talk and walk is too much for my human understanding to take in.'

'She is half Neekan. We talk as soon as we get out of the womb. It is your species that take two years to start talking and walking', Rasirine chuckled.

CHAPTER 22

By midday, Lunette had started to waddle around. Rasirine noticed the look on my face and laughed. 'You'll get used to it'

I smiled and turned back to the fire that would not light no matter how many sticks I rubbed together.

Rasirine left little Lunette to go exploring around the river and came towards me.

'She cannot come with us to the battlefields', Rasirine whispered.

'Why not, Ras? Look at her, by tomorrow, she will be ready to fight.'

'She is not coming with us, and it is final, David!' Rasirine raised her voice at me.

Lunette hurriedly came back to where we were sitting when she heard her mother's loud voice and asked, 'Are you all right, Mummy?'

'Yes, princess, Mummy is fine. How about you help me light the fire?'

Rasirine laughed and said, 'Aw! You are so funny, Daddy! Look at you, trying to light a fire and making mistakes!' Lunette giggled and waddled back towards the lake to fetch me some more dried braches fallen off the trees.

Rasirine gave me an anxious look and was about to start again.

I tried to calm her down. 'All right, do not stress. But just think about what we are going to do? We cannot let someone babysit our little girl, can we now?'

'I was thinking of sending her to Orchadia, to my people.'

'What? You are not sending our child to another planet!' I said in an extremely annoyed manner.

'It is better than getting her killed on a battlefield!' Rasirine responded angrily.

'Well, maybe! But who is going to look after her?'

'The king and queen of Orchadia! My parents, David!'

'Are they really going to have enough time to take care and love a little girl?'

'Yes, they will, David. Do not forget that she is my child too.'

'How did you contact them?'

'I contacted them via my telepathic abilities. They will be here tonight around six o'clock to pay us a visit to meet you and their new granddaughter.'

I was happy and a little bit worried about meeting Rasirine's parents because I did not know what they would think of me. My thoughts went straight to Lunette.

I saw Lunette near the lake. 'No, Lunette, darling. No, do not eat the mud!' And I ran towards her in order to prevent her from tasting the mud that she already had in her hand.

Lunette looked at me in a displeasing manner, but she obeyed my instructions without any resistance. Lunette and I walked back to where Rasirine was sitting. Lunette sat next to her mother and played a game with the grass as I was getting ready to go hunting.

'Go hunt some birds, David', Rasirine said. 'Otherwise, we will not have anything for lunch today.'

I quickly replied, 'I was just thinking of the same thing too'.

'I will see both of my girls in one hour's time.' And I bent and kissed both of them.

As I was walking up to the summit of the hill, I was enjoying the beautiful birds singing from the branches of the trees. I did not want to kill any birds, but I had to if I did not want my Ras and my child to go hungry.

When I reached the top of the hill, I saw a field larger than the river filled with vibrant and colourful flowers of all kinds growing all around. It was absolutely breathtaking. I ran down the other side of the hill, rolling down amongst the flowers.

I cut a few and made a lovely bouquet of flowers for my two lovely girls. I spotted a little gerbil rushing from behind the flowers. I stealthily walked towards it. Its little head looked at me with its big brown eyes and made a little squeak, as if it was trying to beg for my mercy.

I knelt down before it. 'Well hello, little guy!'

The little gerbil first took a few steps back and then a few steps forward towards my hand and smelt it. Then it made a few movements forward and sat in my palms. I picked it up near my face and brought it close to my eyes.

'Nice to see you, Mr. Gerbil.'

The little gerbil squeaked with approval.

'Can I take you to show you to my daughter?'

He nodded his little head as if he understood what I was saying.

'I found some food, and I had some flowers for my favourite girls, and a little gerbil for Lunette to see.'

I ran back up the hill and then down as quickly as I could to get to Rasirine and Lunette. I saw Rasirine from afar holding Lunette in a piggyback, jumping around, and Lunette was enjoying the ride. I started laughing too when I got near enough to them and quickly showed them the gerbil.

'A gerbil!'

'Yes, a gerbil. I founded it over the hill, and some flowers for my lovely ladies.'

'Oh, David, silly little sentimental, David', Rasirine said in a playful mood and asked Lunette to go and have a look at the little gerbil.

Lunette waddled over to the gerbil and asked, 'Daddy, what is his name?'

I did not know the answer to that question because naming little animals was never my forte, and I looked at Rasirine for support. All Rasirine did was to shrug her shoulders and smiled whilst she concerned herself with the flowers.

'Well, I don't really know, Lunette. What do you think we should call him since he will be your pet from now on?' Lunette's face glowed with happiness.

'Thank you, Daddy! I will call it Fish.'

Rasirine looked back at me and fell over laughing till her eyes filled with tears.

'Um, Fish? Is that what you are going to call Mr. Gerbil?' I asked in between laughs.

Lunette looked up at me as if I were an ignoramus who could not understand why on Earth the name Fish sounded silly. She then vehemently responded, 'Yes, this is what I will call my pet. His proper name will be Mr. Fish Flower Gerbil'.

Lunette, clearly happy with her decision on the naming of her new pet, walked off with Mr. Gerbil cupped in her hands. She headed towards the little hut we had made for her from the wood we collected.

I turned around and looked at Rasirine, who was still laughing, wiping the last of her tears off her eyes and said proudly, 'This one will be a troublemaker, I can assure you of that . . . I feel sorry for my poor parents'.

'Let's take a walk to the lake whilst Lunette is enjoying her new pet animal friend', I suggested to Rasirine.

We sat on the edge of the lake, and as we were just about to put our feet into the water, Lunette arrived and sat next to us with Mr. Fish. We spent the day swimming and playing with Lunette and Mr. Fish. It was one of the best days ever. These were the good days before the horrid ones to come.

A large ray of light came down upon the lake. Rasirine and Lunette immediately stopped splashing each other with water.

Rasirine called out, 'It is my parents! It is six o'clock!'

'What? It is already six o'clock? How did the hours pass so quickly?' There was no point for me waiting to get an answer to my questions.

I saw Tarnak and his wife come towards us. They smiled at me and Rasirine.

'Look, Lunette, Grandmother and Grandfather', Rasirine said to our child.

Lunette giggled and ran towards her grandparents. Tarnak picked Lunette up and cradled her. 'Gee, you are a pretty one just like your mother!' he said.

'That is what I said too, sir, as soon as I saw her!'

Tarnak laughed, 'David, my boy, let me introduce you to my wife. This is my wife, Calypso'.

'Hello, Mrs. Calypso.' And I kissed her hand out of respect.

'There is no need to do that, boy. We know who you are. Rasirine has never stopped talking about you', Rasirine's mother said.

I blushed, and Rasirine giggled.

Tarnak took the opportunity to remind both Rasirine and I of the choices available to us. 'We understand that you are continuing your wars, but let it be known that the time is coming nearer. Choose which you will fight first, "the collapse of the universe" or "the war of inequality amongst the species". You must be wise in your selection.'

With that, Rasirine and I nodded and kissed our little Lunette on her forehead, telling her that it was time to join her grandparents in a journey to another planet. Lunette was happy and excited to go with her grandparents.

'Bye-bye, Mummy and Daddy', she called out.

'Goodbye, Lunette', we called back.

Tarnak and Calypso smiled. Before taking off, Tarnak said, 'We will bring her up well. When she is of age, she may come back to help you fight, for words alone of your efforts and sacrifices cannot describe the true courage that you both posses for the salvation of our universe'.

As we watched their spaceship leave, a tear slid down my face. The daughter I had given life to will now live far away from me, in the universe. She will not grow up with us, but she will grow up hearing of us.

I was not feeling happy about Lunette growing up without her parents to stand near her. It was something that I had experienced growing up as a child. I did not want Lunette to grow up feeling unloved because of this war that her mother and I had to fight in order to save the universe.

It hurt me also that my poor little Lunette will have to live alone with the struggle of being a half Neekan and half human, something that I wanted to help her go through in a safe and happy environment.

'She will be fine in Orchadia, David', Rasirine said in an attempt comfort me.

'You do not understand, Ras, my heartache and sorrow.'

'I can read minds when I choose to, and the pain of our daughter leaving us is great for me too. But you know for yourself now, in this war, it is not safe for a child so unique like our own to be with us.'

'What will she be doing on Orchadia?'

'She will be educated and tendered for, and when this is all over, we will go live with her, given that you also wish to join us in Orchadia?'

'I want to be with you and our child, Ras, never doubt that. And I know that our daughter will be kept safe. That is not what I fear.'

'What is it that you fear, David?'

'I fear that our child will grow up with the impression that we chose war over her. She will grow up thinking that her parents did not love her because they preferred to fight in a war and that we are fighters and killers.'

'David, you are too human, and this is what makes you special, but Lunette is also half Neekan, and she will be able to rise above all this.'

'Ras, I want you to understand that I do not wish for our child to see us as people that I do not want her to aspire to be like. I want her to see us as the people who have been wronged by the rest of the universe and that we are the ones who stand up for what we believe in. Who is going to teach her these things?'

'My parents will teach our child whatever she needs to know about us.'

'Yes, I know, but will she understand that we are fighting this war for standing up against my race for the pain they have caused your people? I am not utterly convinced that she will see it like that, Ras. She will see us as the two who saved the universe with war, fire, and pain.'

Rasirine shook her head in disapproval as we were walking back to our tent. 'No, she will not, David. When she sees that my people feel very honoured to have the man who returned to them the most precious book in the universe, *The Secrets of Orchadia,* with her mother, and that they both saved the universe, she will be very proud of us.'

'I cannot wait to live in Orchadia, Ras.'

'You would be king amongst my people, David!'

We walked over to our tent, and as we opened the door, Mr. Fish jumped onto Rasirine's coat. 'Oh, David, I thought Lunette had taken Mr. Fish with her. My parents cannot leave Orchadia again in such a short time and return to Earth.'

I held the little gerbil in my hands, and in a way, I was happy that Lunette left her friend behind so as to remind us of her.

I spoke to Mr. Fish and tried to calm him down, but he was quite distressed, as if he knew that his friend had left him behind.

He was quite jumpy and unsettled. 'Shh! It is all right, Mr. Fish, Lunette did not forget you. It is our fault. Are you going to stay mad at us?'

Mr. Fish stopped jumping around and looked up at me.

Rasirine rolled her eyes and said jokingly, 'May I eat the rat?'

I could not help speaking back to Mr. Fish. 'Mr. Fish, please do forgive my dear Ras. She does not know what she is talking about.'

Rasirine lost patience with me and said, 'You are speaking to the rat?'

Mr. Fish got very offended, so I covered up his ears. 'He is not a rat! He is a gerbil, and he just said that he will not stay mad at us if you promise to not say you will eat him again.'

Rasirine chuckled with embarrassment. 'He heard that, did he?' And she turned to the gerbil and said, 'Sorry, Mr. Fish.'

'He is a gerbil. He cannot speak, and you cannot understand him!' she said.

I turned and whispered to the gerbil. 'Do not worry, Ras is just being silly. Now will you come to sleep? We have got a huge adventure tomorrow! We are going to town, which is near the fields were I found you!'

The gerbil looked at me quite fearfully. It shook its head vigorously.

'What is wrong, Mr. Fish? You do not want to go back to that town?' He squeaked. 'I take that as a no! Why though? Is there a reason?' I asked him.

'Yes!' it squeaked.

'What? Can you please repeat that, Mr. Fish?'

'Bad people, bad town. No go back.' He squeaked louder his response to me.

I was amazed at what I had heard. Mr. Fish had actually spoken! The gerbil had spoken! I ran inside the tent to the sleeping Rasirine, and I woke her up, 'The gerbil he . . . he spoke!' I screamed with joy.

Rasirine sighed heavily. 'Are you for real, David? Please let me sleep. I am exhausted . . . ' And she turned over to continue her sleep.

I sat cross-legged on the floor inside the tent and held Mr. Fish in my hands.

'It is a bad town? Why?' I asked Mr. Fish to explain a little bit better.

'Please refrain from talking to yourself. Honestly, I think you are going mad!' Rasirine angrily responded.

'Sorry!' I whispered, and I took Mr. Fish in my hand and went outside the tent and sat far from the tent where I would not disturb Rasirine and continued my conversation with Mr. Fish.

I asked Mr. Fish once again, 'Why is it bad, Mr. Fish?'

'Bad people know you here. Want to kill you', he said.

I was suddenly frightened. 'How do you know?'

'No, Mr. David. I heard them. They said, "David and Rasirine camp beyond mountain. You are threat to them. They kill intruders. They no want you".'

'What else did you hear them say, Mr. Fish?'

'They will come tomorrow. Fight, sir! Fight with Mrs. Rasirine!'

The gerbil had a little yawn before continuing his sentence. 'I hear because they kill other gerbils too. My family already is dead. I am only one left.'

'Oh, Mr. Fish, you have us now for your family, OK?'

'OK! Mr. Fish knows Mr. David is good man. So I came with you. You must protect you and Rasirine. Good thing Luntti left.'

A fear rose up in me, but I contained my emotions so as not to scare my little gerbil friend and replied, 'Thank you, Mr. Fish, and I hope you won't mind just making a small correction. It is Lunette, not Luntti. But that is all right. You are a wonderful creature.'

The little gerbil did a little roll-over trick in my palm and had a little squeak of happiness.

'No, sir, I call her Luntti, and Luntti calls me Fiss. We are good friends. That is why I will help you.'

I patted him, 'Thank you, Mr. Fish. Thank you very kindly. Good night for now.'

CHAPTER 23

Mr. Fish was unstoppably squeaking.

'What is wrong, Mr. Fish? Are we in trouble?'

'I hear them. They come near now. Wake Mrs. Rasirine up, Mr. David. They are approaching.'

'Do not worry, Mr. Fish. Ras and I are ready to defend you and ourselves. Sit tight and watch the little party.'

'Oh hello! What do we have here? I see guns and pistols you are holding. What century is this?' I sarcastically asked the men and women lined up in front of us, armed and ready to charge.

Mr. Fish was proudly watching from my shoulder, holding on for his dear life.

'How did you know we were coming?'

'I am a human boy who can talk to animals. I am married to a woman who is from outer space, and let's put it simply, I had a hunch.'

'Why did you come to our town anyway?' the guard said, spitting on the ground beside me.

Before I could respond, Rasirine spoke, 'We are here because we came to find our parents. We did not come to cause any trouble!'

The men and women seemed to be less angry with Rasirine's explanation.

Mr. Fish looked at Rasirine strangely. 'Stop putting on that English accent. You tell them, David, we was just here to find my momma.'

My mind was racing at a hundred miles per hour. However, the men and women all relaxed, and Rasirine let out a breath of air.

'How did you all get lost? We are all in England, did not you know that? This is England.'

'Well, we are not actually lost. If you want to see, here are our IDs.'

Rasirine's face glowed with joy, the face she had when she had thought out a plan. She made a signal for me to follow her in the tent.

The townspeople waited the outside whilst Rasirine and I entered the tent.

Rasirine whispered hurriedly, 'Teleport their town, now!'

'We cannot! There is not enough power left, Ras. When we shifted so many times, it used up all the power. It needs solar radiation to recharge for approximately fifteen minutes when the sun rises.'

'Aye! What is taking you all so long?' a couple of angry voices asked from outside.

Rasirine looked at me and responded, 'We are trying to recharge our teleport, and we cannot do this until the sun rises.'

'What is a teleport?' one tall man asked with great curiosity.

'We will show you as soon as we get it charged. Would you like to wait around?' I asked in the calmest voice possible.

'Everybody, put your weapons down!' the leader of the group ordered the rest.

'What are you doing over there?' another question was fired by a woman this time.

'Sorry, we are trying to bring out the devise to show you its structure. Just be patient with us if we are taking some time.'

Rasirine bent over and put three grenades in her armour pockets, and I fitted two laser guns in mine.

'You all want to come and see our village? We just sacrificed one of our men tonight. We are going to have a feast!' the tall man pointed out.

Rasirine and I exchanged fearful looks. I got out of the tent, leaving Rasirine behind to keep recharging the teleport devise.

'You eat your men?' I asked.

'Well, what else have we got to eat? We ate all the gerbils. Except your one, can we have it? We will pay you for it!'

Mr. Fish hid under the collar of my shirt, peeking his little head out for gasps of air. 'You are not going to give me up to them, Mr. David, are you?'

'No, sorry, he is mine. And he is not going to be your dinner no matter how much money you pay for my little friend.'

Mr. Fish was absolutely relieved when he heard my statement.

'Well, all right then, partner, but just so you know, you will not be getting any of our food. You can starve', he said, feeling quite amused.

'We will be fine', I responded.

Rasirine came out of the tent and said to everyone that the teleport will take some time to recharge and it is better to get going. She said in a casual tone of voice that it was not such an important machine to wait around for and missing out on the feast. I knew that Rasirine had a plan.

The leader ordered everyone to head to the town. The man in charge seemed to like us, but everyone else in the group kept a close eye on our behaviour, and one of the men kept an ever closer eye on Rasirine.

'Hey, you blue colour, I really like you. I need someone to look after me because my last wife died of gangrene.'

Rasirine turned and slapped him in the face. 'I am a woman. How dare you speak like that to me?'

All the women stopped and looked at Rasirine. There was silence for a few seconds, and then they all cheered for her.

One of them turned to the man and said, 'She is right! You men treat your wives bad enough. We do not need to deal with your silly wishes. We got our own stuff to do from now on'.

I was so proud of my Rasirine. She was a leader already in a town that did not even know her well yet. Rasirine was the type of a woman who would not let anyone put her down and insult her intelligence.

'And for your information, sir, I am turquoise and not blue.'

'We know what you are. The Turquoise War has been going on for a while now', he retorted.

Rasirine and I pretended that we did not hear him, and we continued walking in silence for what seemed like hours through the grassy fields until we saw the first houses of the town.

'Welcome to Helavia', a sign above the town said. Rasirine chuckled at the name, and a few of the villagers looked at her aggressively.

'You two got a problem with our town?' they asked.

'No, not at all, madam', Rasirine responded with confidence.

One of the men got a little bit too suspicious of us, and he immediately told the leader, who was having second thoughts about us, that it was better to leave us out of town and not to have us as guests for their feast.

The leader turned around and said, 'We cannot have you in our town as guests. My second in charge advised me to leave you out of our town.'

Mr. Fish was very scared because he did not know what was going to happen to us since we were not able to return to our tent safely. After a few minutes of silence, we both calmed down.

The second man in charge said, 'Let's put them in the cave and roll a big rock at the entrance to make sure that they will not follow us'.

Rasirine did not resist, neither did I and Mr. Fish. We were taken to the cave, and without resistance, we entered. It was dark and cold, and no light was able to penetrate through the cave's walls.

When they were all gone, I asked Rasirine, 'Why you did not want us to fight them?'

'It is not wise to alert them. We need to proceed with our plan by eliminating or killing any more humans or anybody else, David.'

'But, Rasirine, how are we going to get out of here?'

'Get out? Oh, do not worry about that! That is very simple! All you have to do is to move back into the cave.'

'Why?'

'Oh, nothing. I am just going to blow it up, and I do not want you to get hurt.'

Rasirine pulled out the grenade from her pocket and pulled me back with her as far as we could farther into the cave before the ceiling became too low to go any farther. We were thirty metres away from the entrance, and the sound of the grenade was so loud that it nearly sent us deaf.

'Ready for launch! Keep Mr. Fish safe under your collar!' she called out.

'We are right next to you, Ras, but Mr. Fish is mortified!'

'I know. I am sorry, Mr. Fish', she said, and she launched the grenade.

'One, two, three!'

I clasped my ears and made sure that Mr. Fish was holding on tightly under my collar.

After a few moments, I opened my eyes only to see Rasirine looking at me in a peculiar way. I looked at her and playfully winked to show my admiration for her that all three of us were safe.

Rock fragments and dust filled the room. The grenade had broken through the rock, but it managed to get us only a small opening that our bodies could not fit through. As the dust was settling around in the room, we were choking from it, which made our breathing even more difficult.

Mr. Fish climbed back onto my shoulder and whispered into my ear, 'You no baby, sir. I baby. I scared'. I patted him and gave him a little kiss on the head.

'Do not worry, Mr. Fish, we will be okay.'

Mr. Fish was so frightened he hid underneath my shirt and was tickling me as he was scurrying around.

'Should I throw the other grenade?' Rasirine asked.

'No, no, no!' Mr. Fish squeaked in fear.

'I do not think so. It might cause the cave to collapse. Look at the cracks in the wall. One more explosion and we are as good as dead! Let's see if we can move the cracked rocks around the opening to make the gap larger to get through', I said, coughing in between every few words.

'OK! I will start from the left side, and you start from the right.'

Rasirine was drawing on all her strength. The weight of those cracked rocks was inconceivable. However, we managed to remove about ten rocks, and the hole was now wider, enough for both of us to fit through.

We moved rapidly through the narrow diastema because it was not safe at all.

'The roof is about to collapse any minute now', I told Rasirine.

'Come on then, get on your stomach and move through the opening.'

'Are we going to crawl through this? What if the ceiling collapses on us?'

'If we die, David, we will at least die together.'

Mr. Fish looked at me and was clearly very scared. Rasirine sighed too and looked at me with an air of agitation and anxiety, which was caused by the imminent danger that the ceiling was on the verge of collapse.

My whole life up to now was marked by this feeling of living constantly in fear.

'I will go first', Rasirine said.

Mr. Fish climbed on top of my head and looked at my face, 'Are you okay, sir?'

'Yes, I am, Mr. Fish,' I nodded and winked at him, signaling everything was under control.

Rasirine was out of the cave, sound and safe. Mr. Fish and I also crawled through the opening and met Rasirine on the other side. We headed back to our tent, running as fast as we could. From far away, we could still see the town's lights, obviously indicating that they were having a big celebration.

'Humans', I mumbled under my breath to Mr. Fish, and he nodded in agreement.

Our tent was over the hill, and we had quite a long distance to go before arriving to it. My mind returned to the first time I met Rasirine when we were running and hiding from one another. Rasirine had this special skill of finding me within seconds where I was hidden.

'You are cheating, David!' Rasirine called out to me, and I suddenly came back to the present moment.

'You read my—'

'Yes, I can read your mind. You went back in the past thinking of the very first day we met, is that not correct?'

'Yes, it is. May I ask you, how do you connect with me?'

'It is called the emotion of love. We are one, David, and I can read your mind. You have been always wondering how I could find you so easily, do you not?'

I nodded as I remembered the time I ran straight off the new bridge of London into the freezing cold water. It was in the middle of winter. I hid underneath the marina docks thinking that Rasirine would never be able to find me. Before I could even lift my head out of the water, there was Rasirine, looking down at me sweating heavily and with a smiling face.

'I found you! David, dear, you really should know much better than to jump off bridges', Rasirine said.

'Ras, reading my mind like that is quite cheeky and intrusive! What if I am thinking about something dangerous, eh?'

'Like what, David?'

'Like . . . like bombing the world!?'

Mr. Fish looked at me fearfully, and I quickly altered my hypothetical intention. 'Do not worry, Mr. Fish, I was just thinking of doing that does not mean that I will actually do them', I whispered to him.

Rasirine chuckled and continued walking off ahead of me amongst the flowery hill. I quickly caught up with her and gave her a big hug that nearly squashed her.

'David, you scared me!' she exclaimed.

'I will race you to the tent', I suggested.

'And what is the prize?'

'Well, whoever gets to the tent first wins, and whoever fails has to jump into the river, walk out, and start dancing like a lobster till the other dies of laughter.'

'I will take you up on this', Rasirine replied with certainty.

Mr. Fish was panicking and begged me by squeaking, 'Please, Mr. David, do not run. I cannot hold on to you, sir'.

'Having second thoughts, do you not think, Ras, that it is a little bit unfair to Mr. Fish?'

'What a poor excuse.'

'It is not a poor excuse at all. Mr. Fish could fall off my shirt collar, and we could be losing him.'

'OK, David, you are right. Mr. Fish is such a lovable and cute creature, and it would be horrible especially for Lunette if we lose him!' Rasirine agreed with me.

Mr. Fish was very happy at the compliment and nuzzled my cheek.

Rasirine was running very fast, and I had to catch up with her. I increased my speed whilst having Mr. Fish constantly squeaking, 'This hurts my head!'

'Do not worry, we are nearly there! Can you see our tent!?' I told him

'Yes, sir, but it is all ripped up.'

When Rasirine and I approached closer to our tent, we both froze. I thought to myself, *What has happened?*

CHAPTER 24

I entered the tent first, asking Rasirine to stay put in her place and to hold Mr. Fish. When I got into the tent, I noticed a note pinned to the canvas which read, 'I have been waiting a long time for a free Neekan!'

There was no name but just the letter S signed at the end of the note.

'Rasirine! Rasirine! Where are you!? Come and see this strange note left in our tent!' I called out.

Rasirine did not respond, and I went out to see where she was. I did not see Rasirine waiting where she was supposed to be. I just saw Mr. Fish nibbling on some seeds.

I went and picked up Mr. Fish and asked him, 'Have you seen Rasirine? Where is she? Why did she leave you all alone here?'

Mr. Fish, instead of answering my question, ran and hid under my collar, chewing on my shirt in fright. 'What is it, Mr. Fish!?'

Mr. Fish did not respond, and I asked him again, 'Where is Rasirine, Mr. Fish? It is important that you tell me because I have found this strange note in the tent and it is all about her. I do not know who left it. It has no name, it has only the letter S, and I am concerned. So please tell me if you know where Rasirine is'.

Mr. Fish scurried back down and around my hands as he jumped from my shirt. 'I knows who S is!' he said.

'Who is *S*? Is this a woman from Orchadia looking for Rasirine?' I asked fearfully.

"Tis not a *she*, Mr. David, it be a *he*! A man!' Mr. Fish squeaked.

'What is his real name, Mr. Fish?'

'Mr. S is very powerful. He took Mrs. Rasirine because he needs her for something very important. I can help you find her if you want me to.'

'Yes, Mr. Fish, you need to tell me his full name so that I can key it in the teleport to locate his exact position on Earth and teleport myself to him to save Mrs. Rasirine.'

'Sir, do not worry about Mrs. Rasirine. She will be fine. You must be armed and ready for his name is one you know and fear.'

'Who is it!?' I yelled at Mr. Fish, who curled himself into a ball.

'Mr. David, please do not yell. I get very scared.'

'You must understand, Mr. Fish, that I need to find Rasirine.'

'Mr. David, the *S* stands for *Sofron*, the leader of the human military force, and now he is the controller of the extraterrestrial enslavement corporation'

'Of course, how come I did not think of it? Who else would it be? I remember his last words in the apartment window: "We will meet again, David, but next time I will win".'

I quickly keyed in his name on the teleport but had great difficulty locating him on Earth. The teleport could not detect Sofron's secret bearings. The signal was coming up as 'unknown'. He could have been anywhere in this whole wide universe having Rasirine enslaved.

Then I turned to Mr. Fish and asked him, 'How am I supposed to find Sofron? Do you think you can help in this urgent situation?'

'Sir, one way you may use is to trace the age of the liquid pen ink he used to write the note with. This will help you determine how far his exact distance is from here.'

'Thank you, Mr. Fish! I am going straight away to apply your suggestion.'

'There is one more thing, Mr. David. You can scan the marks on the ground from his vehicle and the information you will get back will precisely tell you what type of vehicle he used to arrive on Earth.'

I was astounded by the little gerbil's knowledge; its thoughts were exact and feasible, and his responses were logical and cohesive. I noticed also that Mr. Fish's sentence structure in English had improved dramatically and did not miss the opportunity to commend him on his achievement.

'Your English has improved dramatically, Mr. Fish. You are making me very proud to call you my adopted little son!' Mr. Fish squeaked around once more quite happily.

I took Mr. Fish's instructions and went straight to work on them. Then I went outside and tracked the vehicle's marks on the ground. As I was measuring the marks, I noticed the portal was working again, and it gave the specific location of Sofron.

'Mr. Fish!' I called out.

Mr. Fish rushed towards me. He looked like a little brown ball.

'Yes, sir!' he squeaked.

'I found him. Let's go get Rasirine!'

CHAPTER 25

'Ouch! This hurts my head, Mr. David', Mr. Fish squeaked as we were crossing to the other side of the world.

I tried to calm him down by saying that it was not going to last very long; just a few more seconds, and we would be at our destination.

We landed in an old office with cobwebs and dust dressing the overthrown books and the old furniture existing there.

'Sir?' Mr. Fish tugged on my pants.

'Yes, Mr. Fish?' I responded whilst trying to make my way through the filthy office.

'I do not think we are in the right place, sir', he said in the quietest squeak ever, as if he was whispering.

'Yes, I think you are right, Mr. Fish.' And I continued to fumble around the room.

'This is the last place where the flightmobile landed. These are the bearings that the portal specified on the directions.'

'Are you positive, Mr. David?' meekly asked the gerbil.

'I am quite sure of it. The portal's calculations are always correct, and to track a signal so clear incorrectly would be a very serious mistake in the system of the machine.'

The little gerbil scattered around the room, saying, 'I totally agree with you, sir'.

'Are you mocking me now, Mr. Fish? I think—'

Mr. Fish interrupted me. 'No, sir, I am not. I think we are in the right place because I can hear footsteps from far away. I think that Sofron knows you are here.'

'What am I supposed to do, Mr. Fish?'

'For the time being, Mr. David, just get comfortable in a hiding spot because the footsteps are just approaching the door outside.'

'Is Sofron outside the door? Come here then, Mr. Fish.'

I quickly scooped up Mr. Fish into my hands, and we both hid inside the cabinet door. The cabined door had a small keyhole from where I could peer straight at the door and see any movement taking place in the room.

We waited there for a few minutes, and I then asked Mr. Fish, 'You said you heard him arriving? Where is he?'

'Shhh! Just be patient, sir.'

The door opened, and Sofron appeared with his assistant. She was a woman.

I asked Mr. Fish, 'Do you know her name?'

'Shh! Do not talk. They may hear us.'

Sofron yelled at his assistant, 'Do you see him here?'

His assistant was all frightened and did not utter a word but just nodded her head left to right and then right to left again.

'Do not waste my time, you hopeless fool!' he gave her this harsh remark.

I felt sorry for his assistant. It is times like this that I wish my Rasirine was here to teach Sofron a lesson for his arrogant conduct. It is not acceptable to be rude. There is no reason for anyone to be rude to anybody.

Sofron's poor assistant tried to find us by walking behind him like a little puppy following whilst he was searching for us around the room.

'There are no signs that he has been here. Perhaps I have been wrong about you, Marie. I thought you were well trained and talented.'

'But, sir, I cannot understand how I can be so wrong with my investigations.'

'Leave now! Get out. You are no longer working for me!'

'Sir, I do apologise. My machine does say he is present!' the young assistant cried.

'You and your machine are wrong. Get out.'

The young assistant, who could not be more than fifteen years of age, ran out of the office crying. Then I heard faint footsteps, but I was not able differentiate between whether or not Sofron was still in the room.

Mr. Fish was still holding his breath until the last footstep was heard, and he said with sigh, 'I am glad Sofron has left, sir! Can you imagine how dangerous it would have been if he found you?'

I squeezed Mr. Fish's mouth shut. He looked up at me not knowing what was happening. Then we heard Sofron's voice calling out, 'Peek-a-boo! Come out! I know you are here, David. Very clever of you though.'

I did not respond, and Sofron continued talking as if I were right in front of him, 'Tell me how you found me? I am usually quite good at covering up my tracks!'

I felt the nerves rise up in me. I wanted to kill this man, for all the pain he has caused to Rasirine's people and for all the pain he has caused me.

When I saw him through the keyhole, nearing the cupboard, I was getting ready to take him on and surprise him. I jumped out of the cupboard and fisted him with a strong blow of my hand. I knocked him down to the ground and then rapidly pinned him down before he could get up.

As I was holding Sofron down, I asked him angrily, 'Where have you taken Rasirine!?'

His face went purple as I demanded a response.

'She is hidden. You will never find her', he said, gulping for some air.

'Yes, like I would have never been able to find you, but guess what? I have found you, and I have proven you wrong. So you better tell me where you have taken Rasirine. Otherwise, this is the last gulp of air you are taking, and I can assure you I will find Rasirine myself.'

He frowned and looked up at me. 'You? Kill Me?' He tried to release a sarcastic laugh, but he could not because he preferred to breathe instead.

I released his airway passage for a moment to give Sofron the opportunity to talk, but instead he said, 'You would never dare to kill me! Ever!'

'Why would not I?' I asked.

'Because, David, I am your father.'

'No, you are not!' I yelled at him. 'How can a horrible creature like you be my father?' and I broke down in tears. The tears in my eyes were choking me. 'You . . . you cannot be my father! You killed so many Neekans! My father would have never done that! My father is dead! He died like a hero and was not like a hateful creature like you!'

I then released Sofron. He stood up and continued, 'Ah! You see, David, for yourself that I did not die.'

'My father's name was never Sofron. So I do not believe you.'

'Yes, David, I know, but there is something that you do not know. My real name is Solace Tolliday, and according to everyone including your mother, I was tortured and killed for information that was passed on for the protection of the Neekans.'

'So you are a hero as my mother was telling me? How did you become a villain then?'

'Let me tell you. Yes, it is true that I have saved many of the Neekans. I took so many of them into safety and brought them food and water and clothing, but they never appreciated my efforts and the sacrifices I have done for them! They are evil, David. Do not get fooled by them. They have hurt me so much!'

More tears streamed down my face. I turned around and spat at him.

'You are not my father! You are a selfish idiot. I grew up believing that my father was a hero, and I wanted to be exactly like him, to help and protect those who were weak and to give them strength in return. But you have only taken advantage of them.'

'No, David, my boy! You have the story all wrong.'

'You did not save those who were discriminated against! The Neekans are not evil as you have portrayed them. They are only trying to save the universe, and if anyone tries to stop them, they will kill. This does not make them evil.'

'Why are you taking their side, David?'

'I am here to save the universe with Rasirine, and you are stopping me! What type of father would do that to their own child?'

Sofron tried to hug me, but I pushed his hand away, and I got up.

'Do not touch me. You do not mean anything to me!'

His eyes were filled with tears too.

'David, you do not understand, I fell into depression . . .'

'And so you decided to leave your son with a woman who would have to care for me on her own and to do all the things on her own, to live in a society where she was frowned upon and called names? A woman who would work day and night to feed me? You are the man that made my childhood black and terrible!'

'Why are you so bitter?'

'The only thing that drove me to be a good person was my mother's strength. She would tell me all these beautiful lies about you, making you look like a hero when you were not. I do not begrudge her for this because I know what she did and said was to make me happy.'

'Honestly, David, it breaks my heart hearing you speaking in this manner.'

'You lied to me. You have lied to the Neekans, to the press, to yourself, and to my mother. I wholeheartedly despise liars.'

He went to speak, but I did not let him. Years of pain rose inside of me and all I wanted to do was scream and rip his neck apart.

'I never remember you coming to see me! You were leaving me constantly in a world of pain. You never really cared. How do you expect me to understand what you say you went through all these years? You are just making up a story so that you can endear yourself to me, but this is not going to happen.'

'I do not lie, David.'

'My knowledge of you has been full of lies and stories threaded with false information. How do you think I can develop any warm feelings for you and embrace you as my father and accept you after all the things you have done?'

'David, you must understand . . .'

'What? Understand what? Understand how you went on living your life as if I did not exist? Understand and excuse you of how you have lied to me?'

'Please, David, stop it!'

'Seeing you in this state makes me feel sorry for you. I wish I had never met you. You are the one who will never understand how it feels for me first losing my mother because of you and now losing the only person in the world I care about because you have taken her.'

'David, I have been watching you since you were a young boy, and I have been making sure you were safe.'

'When? When was that? When your men attacked my mother? When your bodyguards got instructions from you to lock her up and then come and get me and hit me?'

'I could not help it, David, they were going to kill me and I wanted to be there for you.'

'When? When you broke into my apartment and nearly killed me with one of your blows? I was never safe. I was injured both physically and mentally. I was left all alone to cope with being unloved by my father. How is that making you a good father now? Go on, answer my question?'

'David, please stop it!'

Sofron did not want to answer any of my questions because he knew that I was right with every accusation I was throwing at him.

My eyes red, my body wounded with gash marks from all the fights, my veins pulsing out of my skin, and my tears falling down so quickly with every second I remembered all the things my father had done to me.

'Please, just listen to me', Sofron begged for my attention.

'Fine, you have two minutes, and then you are going to release Rasirine from wherever you have hidden her. Do you understand!?'

'David, I will try and explain the reason why I turned against the Neekans. I was told about your importance to the universe the minute your mother gave birth to you.'

'Then why did you turn against them?'

'You see, your mother was not there when I spoke to Tarnak. She refused to be with a man who was a protector of the Neekans.'

'Why did you not tell her the truth about the Neekans?'

'I had my closest friend Tarnak to sit with at the time. I was trying to be a good person because I was bad on Earth. I tried to do the right thing by the Neekans and Tarnak. He told me that I now had the son that would save the universe and that his daughter would form an alliance with my son.'

'I still do not understand, Sofron? Why did you turn against the Neekans?'

My father paused for a moment and then continued. 'I see from your face that you have met Tarnak.'

'Yes, indeed I have met Tarnak.'

'I tell you now, he is one of the kindest Neekans you shall meet, but there is always the one good apple in the rotten ones.'

I stopped him.

'That is not how the saying goes, Sofron. The saying goes that there is always a rotten apple in the barrel of the good ones.'

Sofron continued by disregarding my remark and pretended not taking notice of my last sentence.

'Tarnak also told me that you had to find a book. The book of Orchadia buried in the secrets of our Earth deep below our surface. He told me that should anyone else try to find the book, they would be stopped in every step they take. He also said that I was not to see you and that only my legend of help should live on.'

'This I do not believe!' I proclaimed in defense of Tarnak.

Sofron wanted to make sure that I was going to change my mind then and there. 'David, I do not want you to believe me, but at least listen. Tarnak said that if I were to bring you up, you would not find the truth for yourself, so he had to distance me away from you.'

'And what did you do, Sofron?'

'I could not do much but to leave you. Tarnak had told me that you were to be the one who was going to change history time and time again. You would be the one who would change the minds of all people and the one who would save the world.'

'I have heard all this before, Sofron. This is what I am actually doing and you clearly know that, so why do you continue telling me what I already know!?'

'It is important, David!'

Sofron stopped and looked into my eyes. I studied his face, and I could tell he was attempting a level of honesty that he had never done before. He was my father. I could see the resemblance in his eyes and mine, but that did not change the feelings of anger I had towards him.

'You may continue', I said, and he nodded.

'Can you remember on your third birthday, when you were playing at the park with Glaron and Rasirine, there was a shadow that you kept seeing but you did not know what was happening?'

I nodded for I did remember.

'Well, the shadow was me.'

I could not resist asking him, 'Why were you coming in the form of a shadow?'

'I had spent some years with the Neekans by that time, and I was not allowed to see you for you had a great mission to complete.'

'How would your presence affect my mission? I could have worked with you and be also under your guidance.'

'Well, there was another reason too. All humans were afraid of me, afraid since I had allied with the Neekans, a species that was considered to be greater than my own. The night, I came home from watching you on your third birthday, it was then that Tarnak had become cruel.'

'What did Tarnak do to you?'

'Tarnak lashed out and told me that I was a failure as a human being, I was a father with no care for my own child, a man who would rather care for his selfish needs rather than to care for the salvation of the universe. He also said that I was a polluted drop amongst the many polluted drops of humans.'

'I understand why Tarnak said that, Sofron, he was losing faith in humanity because of your actions and of the few other human beings.'

'I wanted to be with you and guide you through life with love and proper guidance.'

'Sofron, you were only interested in yourself, and I do not believe a word of what you say.'

'David, it hurts me what you are saying. I was feeling so sad every day that I saw you growing up away from me. I was watching the Neekan families—how happy and joyful they were back on Orchadia—and hatred rose up in me at them for not allowing me to be with you.'

For a moment, what Sofron was saying captured my attention in order to understand why he was conducting himself in the way that he did, and I asked him, 'Why did you develop these ill and destructive feelings when you had the choice instead to seek for me?'

'The feelings of hatred were so strong and unnatural, so evil that I could not stop them and instead I turned against the Neekans. My mistake was that I did waste your life and my life in a shameless and indefensible way.'

'You are still evading answering my question, Sofron. I have to remind you that your days and hours are numbered.'

'You answer my question, David? Do you know how that feels to have your child taken away from you because you have a duty? *Do you!?*'

I immediately thought of Lunette and sadly responded, 'Yes, I do. My daughter is going to grow up away from me. However, I communicate with her on contactogram on a daily basis for hours. I know how it feels, and it is horrible.' I collapsed into my father's arms.

Sofron hugged me and said, 'David, my dear son, our planet Earth is a small world in comparison to the universe, and I know that you have gone beyond your courage and relentless determination to bring equality between the Neekans and humans, but this will never be possible'.

I realised that Sofron had gone through pain, sorrow, and suffering of his own and probably he felt the same heartache that I was going through.

'Sofron, I have a little girl, her name is Lunette. Do you think that she is safe with the Neekans?'

'Your daughter is safe with Tarnak and his wife, she will not be harmed. As I have told you, Tarnak is a wonderful man.'

'Then why do you hate the Neekans so much?'

'Be patient, David, and keep an open mind for what I am about to tell you. I was the Neekans' sole supporter, and I was very proud of that. I was also delighted and felt great pleasure to have a son that would save the universe and fight for the Neekans to the point where I would brag about it to my friends on Orchadia.'

I was attentively listening as Sofron's story was unfolding, revealing information that I never knew before. Sofron mentioned that Tarnak had given him the largest home on land, which made his fellow humans envious of his prosperity and felt resentment at his achievements, possessions, and as they thought, his perceived advantages.

Then I asked Sofron, 'So that made you lose faith in the human race?'

'No, David, that was not the reason. I never lost faith in humanity because of the actions and feelings of a few human beings. I only wanted to support the Neekans because like you, I was determined to create a just universe accepting all the living creatures of our universe without enslaving anyone. It is now that I have turned against the Neekans.'

'You still have not told me the real reason yet', I interrupted Sofron.

He resumed after my interruption. 'Many of the Neekans would whisper lies about you, about how you were to grow up and amount to nothing, and you were to become a half human and half Neekan. You would eventually be a disgrace to their people. In addition, they disclosed that the prophecies were lies even though I had heard them myself. I observed how the Neekans had no compassion and mercy for the liars and cheats. The Neekans would savagely torture any liars and even executing them in front of the other Neekans and mock them as they were dying in pain.'

'This is horrible, Sofron. I just cannot believe that my Rasirine's people are like the way you describe them to be. I am really questioning myself, why should I have faith in Neekans?'

Sofron tried to comfort me by replying, 'I understand, David, why you support them because I too admired and adored this race. But when I saw their evil side, I could not ever see the good in them again. When I was near them, they would speak of the human-Neekan partnership. But when I was away, I heard them speaking in the shadows about how we are vermin and a species that deserves not to live on such a beautiful planet. They are trying to take over because we are more advanced then what they are'.

I was slowly starting to accept Sofron as my father. We sat in the chairs of the dusty room as he was telling me about how the Neekans had wronged him. He said that they took away his rights as a human and hurt him as a resident of their planet. Then he revealed the falsehood in Rasirine's quest of the book *The Secrets of Orchadia* hidden on Earth.

'David, there is no book called *The Secrets of Orchadia*. I have heard their kings and queens in addition to their officials quarrel over the existence of the secrets of their planet in a book called *The Secrets of Orchadia*. There has been no record of such book ever been written.'

I looked at Sofron in disbelief.

'I know you find it hard to believe me, but my advice to you is to not trouble yourself with the book, but you must continue to fight the war. I support your ideals. Not all Neekans are bad. A few polluted drops of Neekans will not make the universe dirty, but do not let them too close to you.'

I held his hand in mine and looked at his long and sad face etched with decades of sorrow, and I decided to call him 'father'.

'Father, do not tell me any more of the book, neither of the wars I will fight in, but instead tell me what you did and what I can do to change it. I believe what you say, and I will help you. Tell me what I need to do. Tarnak has my daughter Lunette and she is a half-Neekan child. For my daughter, I will do whatever it takes to reunite both our magnificent worlds.'

Sofron sounded like my mother when he said that I only had to keep on fighting my battles and follow the road that leads to my ultimate goals of goodness and forgiveness.

I convinced myself that Sofron was not a bad person but rather one who has been misunderstood, and he was deeply hurting.

'I will give you a second chance to prove that you have changed your ways. You must take me to Rasirine. She and I will help you regain your life, and if you like, you can even come with us and fight to make a difference to the universe.'

He shook his head in despair. 'You do not understand, David. The Neekans have changed me! They transformed me into a machine of hatred. I cannot and will not support them! They ruined my life. I have taken Rasirine down, to the chambers. She will sit there for all eternity, contemplating how her life will be now without the one she loves and without her own child. I will not let you go. You will stay here with me. You will have to obey me!'

I stood up, and watching him on the ground crying crocodile tears annoyed me beyond understanding.

'Do not cry and do not start with the lies and the rubbish that you think everyone will believe. It is sad that you utter those lies and what you have turned into. You will never change. Stay here! Stay here and rot in yourself destruction as you have destroyed my life and so many other peoples' lives.'

Sofron tried to reach for the door handle, but I closed it shut. Mr. Fish was silently listening to everything Sofron was saying hidden in my shirt pocket. I locked the doors and the windows and immediately teleported to the chambers.

'Rasirine, Rasirine where are you? Can you hear me?' I was constantly calling out, almost at the end of my endurance.

Travelling across Sofron's cells, I became aware of the numerous vicious creatures he had imprisoned. Some of the creatures with severed arms and legs were dying of infection. My father, Sofron, who was really an evil man, enjoyed seeing creatures suffer.

'David!' Rasirine's voice, echoed lacking strength. I responded with speed in opening the cell where her voice was coming from. I saw Rasirine lying on the floor.

'Oh, Rasirine what has he done to you?' I asked distressingly.

Rasirine was having great difficulty talking, but she managed to say, 'He has beaten me. Sofron is your father, and I know this, David. He is angry with me.'

'Oh, my lovely, do not worry about Sofron. I am here for you.'

'He will not let us live in peace. Sofron thinks that I am the cause of his pain for taking you away from him.'

I stopped her from talking any further and allowed Mr. Fish to greet Rasirine.

Mr. Fish came out of my shirt's pocket and walked onto Rasirine's head and squeaked, 'Mrs. Rasirine, you are a very brave woman. I have to tell you something that happened whilst you were away. I ate your cheese'. Rasirine laughed and wiped away the blood on her arms and legs.

'We have to leave. Sofron will be down any minute, and I do not want to see him.' Before those words left my mouth my father appeared right in front of me.

'You harm Rasirine, and I will kill you this time!' I yelled at him with extreme emotions of pain and anger.

'You would kill me?'

'You evil, loathsome creature!' And I instantly took out my laser gun and aimed it at him.

Sofron stepped forward, and he said, 'I dare you to do that'.

'Do not dare me because I will. You have done with your life. You have been a disgraceful creature who has taken advantage of an innocent race. When you could not use the Neekans anymore, you enslaved them and you hurt them! You were never a hero! You have lied and misled people to do what you wanted. You have fooled my mother too all these years. My mother was talking about you as if you were the greatest person on Earth so she would make me feel special.'

'I loved your mother', Sofron tried to defend himself.

'No, you never did. You gave her up to the authorities, and you have told everybody that she was insane. You will die here today for all the pain you have caused to all of us.'

I pointed the laser beam at him and shot him dead. His body slumped to the ground with a loud thud.

'You killed him!' Rasirine gasped. 'You killed your father?' she said again.

'David . . . ' I heard my father calling me. I ignored him and turned, away leaving him in midsentence.

'It is only fair, Rasirine. He killed me first by leaving me a life of hell through his actions.'

Rasirine and I walked away from Sofron's body as it was lying on the ground. We looked at the other creatures imprisoned, and whilst walking down the dark corridor, Rasirine asked me, 'David, can we please set these creatures free? Seeing them caged like this is so painful'.

'I do not think we can, Ras. Look at them, some of them will be shot as soon as they leave their cages and others will be used as freak-show entertainment. Do you really want them to live a life like that?'

'No, I do not. Let's get out of here, David. It causes me great fear and pain seeing them in this state. What are you going to do with Sofron's body?'

'We will leave it here to rot.'

'We cannot just leave him here to rot . . .'

'Why not? I think it is pretty cool to leave him here in company with the creatures he has hurt and tortured!'

I turned around and looked at Sofron's dead body and asked him, 'What do you think, Dad?'

After a few minutes of walking around the cells, Rasirine and I went back to the old office full of cobwebs and dust. Rasirine asked with surprise drawn on her face. 'Where is the body, David?'

I looked around carefully and responded, 'I . . . do not . . . know . . . It was here a few minutes before'.

'Do you think that your father, whilst he was with my people, acquired the power of regenerating and healing himself?'

I did not respond.

'Here I am! Are you looking for me, my children?' my father answered, walking towards Rasirine and me at a very slow pace.

'You are a . . . you are a zombie! How did you become a zombie? Zombies are not real, and even if they were, you cannot become a zombie within minutes!' Rasirine remarked with anxiety. She then drew her crossbow and aimed it at my father.

'I am not a zombie. Put your weapon down, you foolish girl!' I pushed Rasirine behind me.

'What are you then? How is it that you are still alive!?' I asked him in a perplexed manner.

'I did die, David, so many years ago. Have you forgotten? I had been tortured to provide the authorities with information against the Neekans, and I never did. Tarnak appreciated my loyalty for his race, so he gave me the elixir. This elixir, once taken, does not allow death to conquer the human body! Dying is no longer something I fear', Sofron said in an arrogant and rude tone.

'You are a freak.'

'Not more than you, boy, you are the one who is in love with aliens, to the point where you start wars against your own people.'

'How could I have been so dull witted? It was you! Father had spoken about a man named Sofron, the man who had created the war of the worlds! It was you! You ripped this universe apart!' Rasirine ran towards Sofron in an attempt to hit him in the Neekan way.

'Rasirine, let me tell you that I was always fond of your father. He was an honest man who worried about everybody else and never about himself, and look at him now! Hiding away on his ship, all frightened, and he is trying to save your planet by sending you as his little servant to find the book of Orchadia! Get a grip on yourselves! Tarnak is lying to you!'

'My father is not a liar!'

'Can you not see it!? If there really was a book that would save the universe, why does he not get it himself?'

Rasirine attacked Sofron and pushed him up against the wall with all her strength. Her teeth clenched, and with anger radiating from her body, she looked at him dead in the eyes.

'Never, ever dare to insult the man who saved you.'

Without a care in the world, Sofron took out his Taser and electrocuted Rasirine. She shrieked, and her body slumped down, leaning against the wall. Her hands clutched tightly with pain. I knelt down before her and shook her.

'Ras, Ras, wake up, Ras! Not now! This cannot happen! You cannot die here!' I said, holding back pain as much as I could.

I looked at Sofron with the most condescending look.

'You disgust me', Sofron bellowed, and he continued to be insulting. 'The boy who saves the universe! The boy who starts and ends the war! Ha-ha!'

Sofron continued in a deliberate, frightening tone of voice, 'David, you will never find the book, and you will never defeat me! Look at you, crying over love. You are pathetic. Look at yourself! And you call yourselves warriors!'

Rasirine had sat up and was slowly regaining her strength. I faced Sofron and, in a discontented manner, asked him, 'What do you want? You have had your little parade, you had an audience for your fanciful utterances and big lies. What else do you want?'

Sofron did not have a response to any of my questions. Even the creatures in the prison cells were disapproving of his conduct and grandstanding. All was silent as I looked my father straight into his evil eyes.

'Forget it', he said and walked off up to the stairs.

'Forget what!?' I called after him.

'Everything we have just spoken about.'

His coat was the last thing I saw, and he disappeared.

CHAPTER 26

I woke up next to Rasirine lying on a big green field. All our weapons were neatly stacked and ordered next to the tent. As I looked into the distance, I saw a sign:—'Termination Point'. I sat up alarmed and weapon primed at hand and gazed around. No one was there. Not a single soul, just a sleeping Rasirine under a willow tree. Something was not right.

'Rasirine, wake up!' I poked her body.

Rasirine did not move. I got closer to her and realised that she was not breathing. I put my hand on her forehead and felt that she was not cold. I decided to bring her some water, so I walked over to the nearby pond and tried to scoop up some water. The water was not liquid but rubber and inert. From far away, it looked like water, but up close, it was clearly synthetic.

'Where am I?' I screamed with a fear chilling my bones.

'Where am I?' all around me voices echoed.

'Who is that?' I called.

'Who is that?' the voices re-echoed.

'What is this place?' I asked.

'What is this place?' they responded.

Then I got a reply. 'Ask yourself, boy!' the voices said in unison.

'What!?' I called out.

'What!?' they repeated.

'What did you say?' I asked again.

'What did you say?' the voices returned.

I asked the voices in the vacuum, 'What did you say before you said what did you say?'

The response was, 'What?'

'No, before that?' I clarified.

'Ask yourself, boy', the response echoed.

'Yes, that is the one!' I agreed with the response.

'Ask yourself, boy', the response was repeated.

'Yes, I understand', I said.

'Ask yourself, boy', the voices insisted on the same reply.

'Okay . . . ' I was getting frustrated.

'Ask yourself, boy', the voices kept saying, with every time increasing in loudness, bursting my ear drums. Then they stopped.

'I am a girl.' I recognized that voice. It was Lunette's voice.

'Lunette!?' I called out to the velvet sky.

'Did you hear that, Grandpa? Daddy is calling my name.' Lunette's voice carried out towards the fake horizon.

'Lunette!' Once again, I gave out a long, loud, and piercing cry of excitement.

'Grandpa, I heard Daddy's voice.'

'Luneeeette!' I fell to the ground with tears flowing from my eyes, feeling such an unimaginable pain overtaking my whole body.

'I am not hearing things, Grandfather. I can hear my daddy calling my name! He cannot hear me, and he is very sad. He is crying somewhere very far away. I think my daddy is lost.'

'Lunette, darling, I can hear you, but you cannot hear me. Tell Grandpa it is David, your father, Lunette. I love you, Lunette.' I was greatly frustrated and distressed. I was desperately hoping for Lunette to hear me. If she could hear me, perhaps she would be able save me. My daughter, a heroine before her time had come.

'I am telling you, Grandfather it is Dad.'

'Please do not make me upset, Lunette, it is not your father.'

'Grandfather, why do you have that look on your face? Is my father all right?'

'Yes, your father is fine. I can hear him too.'

'Daddy, can you hear me?'

'Yes, Lunette I can hear you, my darling. Can you hear me?' I asked back as this was my last attempt in trying to communicate with my little Lunette.

My hope of surviving this ridiculous parallel universe was bleak and grim. Then in my despair, I heard Lunette's voice asking me, 'Daddy! Grandfather asks where you are'.

'I do not know. The world that I am circulating in is made out of rubber. Nothing is moving, and time has frozen. I cannot teleport out! Do you think you can ask Grandpa if he can help me?'

'Yes, Daddy, I will ask Grandpa to help you.'

I could hear Lunette asking Tarnak, 'Daddy does not know where he is. Can you help him? He said he is in a rubber world, and he cannot teleport'.

Lunette's voice sounded full of energy and happiness, and she responded, 'Grandfather says not to worry'.

That is a relief, I thought in my head. Not to worry whilst I am stuck in a parallel universe having a two-way conversation with three people.

'Daddy?'

'Yes, Lunette. I am here, and I can hear you very well.'

'Where's Mummy?'

'Mum is here with me.'

'Grandfather said you must count to ten and the time will be distorted.'

I closed my eyes and counted to ten.

I concentrated on seeing Lunette and having Rasirine with me too.

I opened my eyes and I saw Lunette but not Rasirine next to me.

Lunette jumped for joy in seeing me, 'Are you all right, Daddy? I am so happy to see you again.'

'Yes, I am all right. Now tell me, how have you been?' I called out a little too loudly. 'Oh, Lunette!' I picked her up and held her in my arms.

Lunette was all smiles and gave me a kiss on the cheek.

'I missed you, Daddy.'

'I have missed you too, Lunette.'

'Daddy, when you feel a little bit better, do you want to play with me? I want to show you the dolls that Grandpa made for me.'

'Of course, sweetheart. Give me a moment with Grandfather, and I will be with you very soon.' She giggled and hopped off into her room. 'Little Lunette has grown so much. Thank you, Tarnak.'

'That is all very well, she is my granddaughter also, and I do adore her, but there are greater matters at hand. Rasirine has contacted me telepathically. She is safe. She will be coming here within the next hour or so. She is taking the long way.'

I was relieved hearing that Rasirine was well and safe.

Tarnak and I spent some time talking about the adventures that Rasirine and I had faced so far in pursuit of the book. I told Tarnak about Sofron and how our encounter was not a pleasant one and how Sofron was telling me all these lies about Tarnak.

Tarnak was extremely offended about what Sofron had said about him. 'David, you have met your father and you have met me. You are married to my daughter, and you are old enough to be able to distinguish who is telling the truth and who is not.'

'Tarnak, your deeds and kindness has helped my people. I have chosen to believe you, and I will fight for you, for your people, and most importantly for your daughter and your granddaughter.'

Tarnak smiled and was very happy with my response. However, something was eating me about what Sofron had said about him, and I decided to ask Tarnak the question in hope that I would not offend him.

'Tarnak, may I also clarify something with you that really bother me about Sofron?'

'Please, David, go ahead and ask me.'

'Sofron told me that you had forbidden him to see me. Is that correct?'

'I will tell you the truth. I did forbid your father from seeing you because of the man he is. He was going to harm you and your people by blaming us. We knew what type of person he was, and we had to keep him under tight supervision. It was better than letting him wild and free.'

'I understand, Tarnak, but do you not think that it was a bit harsh what you did?'

'David, he was going to destroy planet Earth and the universe, and I am just about to answer your next question about the elixir.'

I looked at Tarnak with surprise, and he said, 'I know what you were going to ask me, David. Has Rasirine not told you about our mind-reading ability?'

'Yes, she has, but I thought it was only Rasirine's ability.'

'No, all Neekans have that ability.'

'What about the elixir that you gave my father?'

'Not to worry, it will not last long. Your father is ageing, and we have our tabs on him.'

I had so many questions to ask, so many thoughts and ideas buzzing through my mind. I thought through all the ones that I could think of, but the most pressing one came to my mind, and here I was with the man who could answer basically all the things that I ever could have a query about.

I asked a final and the most important question that was turning in my head.

'Why was I the one chosen for this mission to save the universe, Tarnak?'

'Well, I cannot answer that question, David.'

'Why not? You know the answers to everything! You are a genius!'

'Ah! See, David, I am not a genius. The qualities you see in others are the ones that are reflected in yourself! What has been happening to your subconscious up until now is all Sofron's work.'

'Why? I am supposed to be his son. Why would he want to hurt me?'

'Sofron used your strong love for Rasirine to get you back to him, by hiding her from your present environment. He wanted you to lose faith and think that Rasirine was not going to be with you any longer and her absence will cause you to suffer for eternity.'

'Sofron is an evil man, and it hurts me because he is my father.'

'Do not hate him, David, for Sofron had never felt the strong love that can exist between father and son.'

Tarnak's words were filled with much wisdom and honesty. I now understand the reason for my father's rage towards Rasirine and me. It was because he had never been loved and he did not love anyone in his life. He was a dead person on the inside, and that was what drove him into being a bad person.

Then Tarnak said, 'David, your strong love for Rasirine and your daughter made the telepathic connection strong enough to travel thousands and thousands of lightyears to get to the ones you love'.

In the distance, I could hear Lunette calling out for me. I had forgotten the promise I made to her that I was going to join her to play with the dolls that her grandfather had made.

Tarnak had a strange look in his face, and he looked as if he was going to doze off for no apparent reason. And then he said with no prior connection to what we were discussing, 'Go and sit with your daughter because you will not have many years together!' And his eyes rolled back into his head.

I was terrified not knowing what has come over Tarnak. He looked as if someone was directing his speech or that he was hallucinating. Tarnak looked at me, not remembering what was going on, and then he said, 'Pardon me, just dozing off again. Is that my granddaughter Lunette calling me? Where is my daughter Rasirine? I will wait for her, and you go with Lunette to see her dolls.'

Then Tarnak sat down exhausted, and before he dozed off, he said, 'Next time, *I will win*!' And he fell into a deep sleep.

I thought for a moment Tarnak was probably tired, so I decided to let him be and went into Lunette's room to see her dolls and play with her as I had promised.

CHAPTER 27

I entered Lunette's room, which was full of different toys and dolls made by Tarnak. As soon as Lunette saw me, she excitedly jumped up and said, 'Daddy, you finally came. Why did you take such a long time?'

'Lunette, sorry for being a little late. Grandfather and I were having a very serious talk about the universe.' Lunette smiled at me and then pulled me by the hand to sit down with her.

'That is all right, Daddy I understand. Grandpa has told me about Sofron and how nasty he can be.'

'Really?' I asked little Lunette.

'Yes! I wanted to see Sofron too, but Grandpa said that he was dangerous. Have you seen Sofron, Daddy? Do you know what he looks like? Does he have a big head and yucky little cockroach eyes? Is he smelly?'

I laughed as I was listening to her innocent questions; her childish naivety warmed my heart and made me smile. I sat down next to her on her bed and decided to tell her about Sofron.

'Well, he is smelly, and he is so very big! He always wears a black coat, and his face is scarred with a big cut on his left cheek. Indeed you were right imagining him having yucky little cockroach eyes.'

Lunette broke into a fit of giggles and rolled on her bed. She had a huge room with her own Portal Pod and a six D television.

Then Lunette pointed at one of her dolls and said, 'Look, Daddy, this doll laughs when I laugh'.

'Did Grandpa make this doll?' I asked, amazed at Tarnak's talent.

'Yes, and look at this one too. This doll cries when I cry.'

I really liked the dolls that Tarnak had made for Lunette. It was interesting seeing them respond to emotions and moods.

Lunette's room was decorated with flying spaceship, glittering stars, colourful planets and galaxies drawn all over the walls. A short gentle knock on the door interrupted Lunette and me.

It was Rasirine. 'You two are having fun there, I see!'

Lunette ran to her mother's arms and started kissing her on the cheek.

'You have grown so much, Lunette!' Rasirine said as she was surprised with our daughter's height. Then Rasirine gave me that familiar look signifying, 'We need to talk'.

'Lunette, Mum and I need to have a little chat about what to buy you for your birthday. We need to spend some time together, and then she will come to play with you, princess.'

'Okay, but please do not worry about buying me anything. I have everything I could possibly ask for already.' She gave a polite smile and went off to play with her dolls again.

Rasirine and I walked outside. 'What happened?' I asked.

'I do not know. Something very strange happened that I cannot explain.'

'Rasirine, do not worry.'

'Why did you leave me, David?'

'I did not leave you. It was Sofron who has the ability to enter my mind and travelled me to a parallel world in my head.'

'Sofron will keep coming back to us. He does not like me, David. I am really worried about you.'

Lunette came out of her room, dragging her dolls to show them to Rasirine. We kept silent for a few minutes, and then Rasirine asked Lunette to go back to her room. Rasirine turned to me.

'David', she whispered.

'Yes?' I asked

'The war is about to begin', she said with sadness.

'I know, Sofron had told me that this time, he will win. He broadcasted the news all over the universe. He said that his men and women will fight, and there is no going back.'

Rasirine was even more terrified. I tried to pacify Rasirine by telling her that Sofron's army will turn on one another since they are lacking love and had only anger permeating them for the rest of the universe.

'Sofron has supplied his army with strong weapons. Do not forget that he was with the Neekans for quite some time and he has learnt our sophisticated ways of using the laser beam guns.'

'Rasirine, do not worry. Sofron's human weaponry is weak and pointless. We have the upper hand.' And I held her hand.

'David, I have faith in you because I know that you will survive to save Orchadia.'

'You will fight with me, Ras.' I looked at her loving eyes that resembled diamonds reflecting light under the moonlight.

'I am saving not Orchadia without you, all right?' I told her.

Rasirine's eyes filled with tears.

'You cannot do that, David, if something happens to me, you must—and I know that you will—go on without me. You should not allow anything to keep you back from your mission. I am here for you now. But if something happens to me, you must go on. Promise me, David.'

'What are you saying, Ras?'

'Promise me for Lunette's sake and for the rest of the universe?'

I nodded my head with sadness. I looked at Rasirine, and she was dozing off like Tarnak, and I heard saying, 'I will win!' And she went to sleep.

'Ras, what did you say?' I asked her as she was dozing off.

'I did not say anything, David. Are you all right?' she said in a voice totally awake tone of voice.

This is strange, I thought to myself.

Then Sofron's voice echoed in my head. 'Beware, you cocky fool, beware!'

CHAPTER 28

'Move and you are dead, you got that?'

Rasirine and I froze. We did not know what to do. We tried to see whose shadow the reflection was, but we could not. I was pointing my laser beam gun towards the shadow, and Rasirine went behind the wall and was also aiming at the shadow.

'Oh, is this how you are going to treat a good friend of yours?' And we saw Glaron popping out from behind a tree.

'Glaron!' Rasirine and I excitedly called out, and we ran and embraced him. y

Glaron was my best friend and an individual who appealed both to all Neekans and to me because of his higher instincts and aspirations for a better universe.

'You are early!' I said to him.

'No! You are late!' he responded to us.

'No, look at this letter! Did you not receive one?' I asked Glaron, and before Glaron could answer, Rasirine immediately produced a letter, which had gone to all the Neekans, informing them about the precise time to open out in space from Orchadia with ten spaceships and then to Earth for the attack.

As Glaron was looking at me with surprise, I said, 'No, we are not late, Glaron. Just have a look at the instructions and the warnings in the letter!'

Glaron snatched the letter out of Rasirine's hands. He read the letter carefully and then looked at Rasirine and me and said, 'OK! I presume I was a little bit too eager to start fighting'.

'You are fine, Glaron. We are very happy to see you after such a long time', Rasirine said.

'I am happy to see you too', Glaron responded, all excited.

Rasirine detected Glaron's keenness to fight in the Turquoise War, but as a princess, she did not tell her people that the book with the secrets of Orchadia was nothing else but to fight without weapons to implement justice in the universe.

'What is our next move? Are we ready for the all-out attack?' Glaron asked impatiently.

Rasirine and I shook our heads with mixed feelings of sadness and excitement and responded, 'Yes!'

'What is happening with you? Why are you both so gloomy?'

'We are not gloomy, we are just thinking of our daughter Lunette who is going to be growing up away from us. We have not had enough time to spend with her. The destruction of the human force is not really to our benefit, Glaron', Rasirine proclaimed.

'One moment . . . is it not the case that we are trying to save Orchadia from burning to ashes and then the universe?' Glaron asked with definite confusion vibrating in his voice.

'Of course, Glaron, the real war begins tomorrow! We are waiting for the space station to send us a message on contactogram.'

'What do you mean the real war, David? I am really tired waiting around for this war to take place.'

It was obvious Glaron was tired—tired of the strife he had gone through, tired of the pain and hurt he had experienced every day of his life.

'Listen, Glaron, first we need to get to the control room, which is stationed in London.'

'How are going to do that? The control room is huge and very well guarded by the humans.'

'Based on the instructions we have from Orchadia, the humans have spaceships that are relatively small in comparison to ours', Rasirine said.

'What are we waiting for, Rasirine?'

'We are waiting for the orders and the signal to commence attack any minute now', I said to Glaron.

Glaron was still very impatient and said, 'David, listen, as I was travelling through the galaxies to get to Earth, I saw three human space stations attacked by the Neekans'.

'Where was that?' I asked.

'It was in the orbit between Mars and Earth', Glaron responded.

Rasirine said, 'We only need our laser beam guns David. One bolt and it sends the human spaceship into pieces. Our spaceships can carry up to fifty Neekans.'

I could not help thinking like a human, and I said, 'Rasirine, Glaron, I am wondering if this Turquoise War is really going to bring a "new world for justice" amongst all species in the universe. Why don't we fight just for the salvation of Orchadia by first finding the book and then engage in war if that would be necessary?'

Glaron and Rasirine kept quiet for a moment and then Glaron said, 'I am really tired. I suggest we go back to the tent and regroup, relax, and then think about it again'.

'That is indeed a good idea', I said, and we all teleported back to the tent.

Glaron decided to have a rest. Rasirine and I could not go to sleep, so we looked through the peephole to outer space. We observed the thousands of stars sparkling in the darkness, and we were thinking of the civilizations existing in the other galaxies so many lightyears away.

It was a breathtaking experience imagining 'us' being here, on Earth, trying to fight a war for a new 'just' universe to prevail. We are so small, so disproportionate and unimportant to the rest of the universe. Yet we think we are so amazing just because we have some robots, laser beams, radiation, and spaceships to travel through time and distances of lightyears at such a high speed.

Rasirine and I were constantly checking on contactogram throughout the night for any messages arriving from the Neekan's space station. Finally, in the early hours of the morning, we got an update that all social media networks of the human world such as television, radio, and Internet were broadcasting the announcement of the Turquoise War taking place today.

The media had convinced humans that the Neekans were a great threat to planet Earth and 'out of fear', men, women, and children were arming themselves with all kinds of weapons.

The Neekans were not afraid as they would enter the battlefield by implementing the most sophisticated war techniques. This war against humans was not going to endear the Neekans to humans. The orders from the Neekans were 'shoot anyone who has not got the mark'. Giant robots were to invade planet Earth.

Glaron woke up and called out, 'The robots are here!'

Rasirine and I ran to the tent. 'What is happening, Glaron?'

Glaron showed us the teleported images on his device of ten giant robots entering the city of London.

'Let's go!' I called out to Rasirine and Glaron.

'Rasirine, teleport us to the control system of the city immediately!' And she did.

Those gigantic machines were not welcomed by humans, and they started panicking. *If this is how they are going to react*, I thought to myself, *there is no need to have this Turquoise War. The Neekans have already taken over.*

Rasirine and Glaron directed the robots via their handheld controls, and Rasirine called out, 'David, follow the robots to enter the control system of the city'.

I was terrified of these monstrous masses of tin. A guard ran up to one of the robots, and at a metre's distance, he tried to shoot it down. 'You iron toys!' he yelled and kept firing his gun.

When he ran out of ammunition, through his useless persistent shooting, the other three guards joined forces to save him from the robot. One of the guards actually clanked onto the robot with menace. Then the police and the army followed since all the alarms had gone off.

'Sir, enter control room. Safety is checked!' the robot spoke to me.

Some policemen and soldiers who were still fighting the invincible robot thought that I was directing the robot, and they tried to shoot me, but the strong sensors on the robot built a protective magnetic field around me so that I could accomplish my task.

'David, get down!' Glaron's voice went through the magnetic field and reached me.

'Nearly there!' I responded.

All we wanted was to make a difference, to make our universe a better place and influence the men and women of planet Earth in having a harmonious cohabitation with the Neekans. The resistance of from my fellow humans was frustrating our dreams in this futile Turquoise War.

One of the guards yelled at the other guards, 'Run! Run!' And they ran down the road instead of jumping in the flightmobiles and taking off.

This is why it has taken humans thousands and even millions of years to understand basic concepts and advance further. Once electricity was discovered, humans learnt more in one hundred years than what they had learned in two thousand years.

One of the guards fell whilst I was entering the control system. No one came to his rescue.

I heard Glaron's voice. 'Come on, David, you have learnt the most important things for this war. Shut the system down. You will not die.'

This is the potential of the humans, I thought and quickly answered Glaron, 'I am not afraid to die, Glaron, but this war is wearing me down!'

'Get going and I am sure humans will understand at the end of this war.'

Then I heard Rasirine's voice echoing through the building. 'David, do not be afraid! You are very intelligent. Just apply what you have learnt from the Neekans.'

'Ras, no offence, but what I have learnt so far has not helped me solve the profound mysteries of the universe.' Rasirine did not respond.

I proceeded and arrived at the main control room. The robot now took over and put all computers into a state of malfunctioning. This was it. My mission was accomplished even though my ability to think on my feet was diminished.

My greatest fear was how to convince and help humans to accept the message of learning to get along with the Neekans. My mind became like the computers. I was not able to think of anything.

Rasirine gave me instructions. 'David, leave the control room now and the robot will protect you on your way out to join us.'

'Do you think I will be able to do it, Ras?'

'I know you can, David, and you will do it for Lunette.'

This seemed to be the most important task that I had to finalise, and I did. The robot assisted me on my way out and helped me get back to Rasirine and Glaron. I saw another guard falling off the steps in his attempt to capture me whilst firing at the robot. Then more soldiers came to his rescue, but the magnetic wall made the soldiers collide into one another.

'Welcome back, Chief in Command!' Rasirine said in a playful tone of voice, and her body language enhanced her talk by standing tall in front of me.

'You made it back, David. Well done.' Glaron praised me too.

I became tongue tied and did not know what to say. I could not understand why Rasirine and Glaron both marveled at my achievement when it was them who had encouraged and helped me overcome my fear.

Glaron looked bored and restless, so Rasirine ordered, 'Glaron, get all the robots back and teleport them back to our Space Station'.

'Of course I will do it. I forgot about the robots because I was waiting for David to say something, but look at him, he is engaged in too much human thinking.'

Rasirine came to my defense and said to Glaron, 'It is not a matter of David's thinking, Glaron. This is the human's way. When human women and men have important ideas, they keep them to themselves rather than share them. They want to be sure before they express their ideas'.

I then asked, 'What are we going to do for the book, Rasirine?'

Glaron teleported the robots whilst listening to Rasirine and me; then he looked at me and said to Rasirine, 'Without this man, we would not be able to find anything! Our Turquoise War would have been impossible without him!'

Rasirine agreed, 'Certainly, David's help was extremely essential'. And she went further to explain to Glaron, 'It is not about the Turquoise War, Glaron, it is about creating a better future for our children. Sofron started all this. He created this war within our people and caused immense pain both to humans and Neekans. I am merely here to end it'.

Glaron got a message on contactogram that the greatest of the Bormindians will be fighting with us for the freedom of the universe.

'Who are the Bormindians?' I asked

'The Bormindians have red skin, redder than blood', Glaron responded, and then he sent an affirmative message to them. They were teleported beside us within minutes.

Thousands of our finest men and women arrived within a few moments. The Bormindians gave us some ideas and we instantly applied them. With the Bormindians' techniques, we were able to devise a better strategy for the impact.

Klowaottle was the Bormindians' leader. He approached me and bowed. 'The man who saves the universe. You shall lead us into battle, and you shall help us do the best for the worlds we are fighting for.'

I was shocked, but at the same time, it was an exciting and satisfying experience.

'You do not need to do that, sir. You are much more of a hero then I will ever be, for you have come here to fight a war that is not your own!'

The leader stood up to salute me, and it was only then I realised that he was as tall as a giant, more than seven metres tall. He had an authoritarian voice as he coordinated his army with their enormous sonic power weapons.

The city with its human defence, army, and other forces would never be able to defeat the Neekans with so much power.

We marched, through the fields, for hours before reaching our target point. Rasirine was walking beside me as we led our people through the forests. No one spoke; they were preparing themselves for what was to come. The Neekans protected their heart as much as they were able to because if they were shot in the heart, their healing powers would not work. An injured heart, Rasirine has said is a condition that cannot be remedied.

I was admiring the army's confidence, displaying true bravery and valour as we were marching through the fields. Rasirine spotted an apple tree, and she quickly reminded me, 'David, do you remember when the humans were on the moon, the astronauts as you call them, the very first food they ate was applesauce?'

'Ras, how does the Neekan mind work? Here we are, going to war, and you are thinking of all these things relating to humans.'

'I know, David. It is a bit confusing to you.'

I am trying to get my thoughts together and put them in a logical order but cannot. How could I be the head of this army? I wondered.

'This is natural for humans, David. There is no logical order in many of the things that you think and do. For example, you humans invented the automatic pop-up bread toasting machine and before that the bread slicing machine.'

'How are you sure that you will win this war, Ras?' I asked.

Rasirine was quick to explain. 'Firstly because we have you as a human helping us, secondly your people are afraid of death. Humans are afraid of losing their life. We are not because we have superior healing powers. The universe is in danger because of your father Sofron who has turned against the Neekans and wishes to burn Orchadia and then rule the universe.'

Glaron called out to the army, 'Only two kilometres to go!'

Then Sofron's voice sounded from nowhere. 'Do not be afraid, boy, for you will die today. Then Rasirine will die too. I have told you that next time, I will win! Now go on! Start your war. Remember, I am always watching.'

I turned to Rasirine who was tired and sweating. 'Rasirine!' I said in fear. 'Sofron spoke to me again in my head. He said first he will kill you and then me. Please contact Tarnak to teleport you back to Orchadia'.

She turned to me and looked into my eyes. Then she stopped walking and announced to the rest of the army, 'Sofron, the great evil plague of the universe, has come once again to David's mind and told him that he will win this time'.

I expected everyone to shout with glee at how we were to defeat him, but they did not.

'Let us win!' a little girl cried out. I seemed to have heard her voice quite easily as if she was speaking to me. I immediately recognised her voice. It was Lunette's voice.

The army looked at her and responded to her command, 'We will win!'

'We will win!' every single warrior called.

'Target approached!' Glaron called.

Glaron came closer to me and whispered, 'Tell them now is the time to fight. You are the leader, you must tell them'.

I am a man of conviction, and I shall lead my army, I thought to myself.

CHAPTER 29

Humans jumped out from inside their homes, screaming and holding their children. Terror and fear spread across their faces. They ran as fast as they could.

'Separation for A, B, C!' I called out.

Our colossal army spread apart in a perfect formation towards the city.

Glaron, Rasirine, and I were in row A. We entered the city. Grenades were thrown towards the complexes. Men and women of all different kinds were coming towards us with guns and knives and rocks.

Rasirine and I led our group into battle as we ran headfirst into the fight. Roars of pain from both sides as knives pierced skin with ease and gun bullets penetrated skin, flesh, and bone. My fellow humans, men and women, were falling and dying in multitudes.

I grabbed a man's arm that was coming towards me, viciously pointing a knife. I looked at his wrists. He didn't have the mark. I sighed and drew my gun. I zapped the man; his body flared with the electric shot and plummeted to the ground.

The war continued on. Blood was spilling everywhere, necks were being wrung by bare hands, people's legs were sliced off—gruesome fights continued for hours and hours till late. The sun began to set upon London, and the humans backed away as night fell. They knew with no power and no weaponry, night was not the time for their petty human fights as we watched them leave still armed and still ready for a quick change of plans. They left and hid away in fallen and burnt buildings, running and crying to their families for their loss.

I asked ten young soldiers filled with pride and strength to keep guard on the borders. 'You watch the borders of the camp for the next hour, and I will send another shift to take the next watch in an hour.'

The rest of the army had rest until their shift came up. I walked over towards Rasirine and Glaron, and we entered out tent. Everything was set up nicely, and the little food we had left was rationed between the soldiers.

The next day, the same ugliness continued. My path was cleared as my men, women, and children—the warriors of the universe—ran towards victory, flattening everyone in our way. Limbs, body parts, heads were being sliced off and scattered everywhere. Hundreds of bodies were bleeding laid amongst the dirt and the rubble.

Teams B and C had destroyed the towers and the business centres; bombs and grenades fired from every direction at the city people. Screaming, anger, pain, fear, disaster was everywhere. Most humans ran inside their homes and locked their doors as if little pieces of metal with no value would save them from their own choices!

'Daddy . . . ! I am lost . . . ! Where are you?' I heard Lunette's voice asking me.

I gasped loudly and turned to Rasirine and asked her, 'Where is Lunette?'

She looked at me and responded, 'I thought she was with Glaron!'

We both glared at Glaron, and he said, 'She told me that she was going to join you!'

'And you let her out of your sight!?' Rasirine released a paralysed maternal scream, one of pain and loss. 'She is only a child! How did she get here in the first place?' And she rapidly forged ahead.

My heart doubled its pace of beating at the very thought that Lunette was lost and seeing Rasirine engaged in this extensive search for Lunette. Rasirine's eyes glazed through her tears and yelled, pointing and glaring at me accusatively, 'David? You brought Lunette here!'

I was very upset too and responded, 'This Turquoise War may have brought me an exhilarating feeling, but I can assure you that I would have never risked Lunette's life.'

The Bormindian soldiers stood still. Not a single word was uttered. Then with an abiding courage, they started singing a song in a language, which sounded magical and unique. I thought about how lovely it would be for Lunette to also hear it.

Rasirine ceased shouting, and everyone turned to look at the tall giants. They were emitting a strange light of silver through their bodies as they sang. And as every note flew past gracefully and melodiously, it became stronger and much more vibrant than before.

Lunette appeared in the distance, rising at a slow pace towards the air, and then she was lifted at the same pace high up in the sky with her clothes drenched in blood. As the silver light from the Bormindians' song was getting stronger, Lunette's still and lifeless body was redirected down into my arms.

I opened my arms and held Lunette's body, trying to contain my deep emotions of sadness, for Lunette was a child that would delight any parent. She lay in my arms for a few moments, motionless, as her wounds and scars started to fade. Her clothes were cleansed from the stains of the human blood, and for a fleeting moment, I thought she would open her eyes too, but instead I saw that tears flowed from Rasirine's eyes. Tears never before so concentrated with pain and hurt.

'My child!' she cried. All the soldiers, both men and women and even young children, knelt down and prayed to their different gods and goddesses for Lunette.

Humans had lined the streets, trying to capture the scene as if it was a side show. Rasirine was inconsolable. 'My child is dead! My child has died because of you, vermin humans! Have you not had enough of hurting my people day after day?'

I looked down at Lunette's face, a frown and a tear was frozen upon her porcelain skin. Rasirine bent down to kiss Lunette's forehead as I was holding her. Then she ordered the Bormindians, 'Send her to my father, to the king of Orchadia, King Tarnak. If you send her fast enough through the lightyears, King Tarnak might be able to save my child.'

Lunette's body rose from my hands and disappeared from our sight within moments. I was in misery and stricken dumb for a millionth time of what these outer space creatures were able to do. I was certain that no matter what, Lunette would be safe. Tarnak would employ all his Neekan power to save his granddaughter.

The humans were growing in numbers, marching towards us. This time, a woman was leading the battalion of various soldiers and warriors. When she was close enough, she stopped and singled out herself from her army and marched forward to speak to us. Rasirine and I looked at the woman leader straight in the eye.

The woman said, 'You came here and destroyed our planet Earth! Why did you do that! We were frightened this is why we killed your child!'

Rasirine's turquoise veins were popping up against her turquoise skin, and she angrily said, 'You wanted to win the war so you attacked my child. We did not kill any of your children, you vermin race!'

'Why did you come to planet Earth then?' the woman leader asked more calmly this time.

Rasirine responded with the distinction of a brave mother and commander. 'We came here to find the book that would save the universe and our planet Orchadia from burning into ashes. This book was planted in the deserts of your planet because my people, the Neekans, had great respect for humans and they thought that *The Secrets of Orchadia* would be safe in your planet.'

'Are you saying—and expect us believe—that you came here to save us and the universe?' the woman leader asked with an air of irony and disbelief.

Rasirine was boiling with anger at the insolence of this woman leader and responded, 'We came here to save you, but not anymore'.

Rasirine ran, stepping over the dead bodies with her crossbow in her hand, shooting hundreds of arrows per minute towards the woman's army. Screams of humans echoed everywhere. Fear and terror rose in all of us, but we stood strong. The rest of the army followed Rasirine.

Teams B and C called over on the intercom to let us know that they had surrounded the whole human army and were waiting for further orders whether to exterminate them or not.

I gave the following orders: 'Separate those with the mark, exterminate the rest of them.'

Not one of them had the Neekan mark; they all hated us. My laser beam singed holes in my fellow human's arms and bodies. They howled with pain at our weapons and snarled at us whilst moving back. They had become rabid like diseased and plagued dogs.

Sofron's voice came back in my thoughts and said, 'My soldiers would win!'

'Sofron, get out of my mind. You are the cause of this Turquoise War. You are so ruthless that you even killed my daughter.' I was livid by that time with him.

'Do you really think I would fall to such a shallow level as to have your daughter killed?' Sofron's voice echoed in the background.

'I am right here, David. I am no longer in your thoughts', he said.

I turned to the left, turned to the right, looked up and down 'Where? I cannot see you', I said with my teeth clenched at Sofron's stupid mind games.

'Oh, my dear David, I am everywhere', he whispered into my brain.

Then he yelled, 'Watch out, son!'

A wild human ran towards me with his gun and shot me. The metal bullet pierced the skin of my shoulder and went right through the bone and flesh and stopped on the back side of my shoulder.

'Leave me alone, Sofron! Let me fight this war without your supposed warnings!' I yelled.

I looked around and saw my men were falling one after the other. It was definitely Sofron and the human's rage that was building as they ran towards us again. The human army was advancing at a quick pace after their retreat. They were shooting with their guns, piercing the Neekans' skin at an incredible rate.

Rasirine screamed with pain but continued on with valour. She shot arrows everywhere, piercing the eyes and necks of many humans. The atmosphere was filled with roars and howls of pain. Little children ran out of their homes, crying as they saw their mothers and fathers dying before their eyes.

I shouted to Glaron over the clashing of the guns, grenades, and roars of the soldiers, 'Take the children and keep them safe!'

Glaron ran towards to the children and instantly beamed them safely to the Orchadian spaceship in the Neekans' space station orbiting Pluto.

Human and Neekan bodies were scattered everywhere. The roads of the city had turned into rivers of human and Neekan blood.

CHAPTER 30

I was spinning through space. By now, my head should have exploded, but it did not. It seemed like I was everywhere and my insides were churning. We were in 'normal time-reversal symmetry', the Neekans said. I asked Rasirine to explain what that meant, but she shook her head and said, 'You will not understand, David. We are travelling through time and space.'

'What do you mean that I will not be able to understand, Ras?'

'You humans do not care much about science! Unless the information has a sexual content or is related to famous humans . . . that you call them "celebrities", you won't bother to learn about it.'

'I am deeply offended, Ras. You are forgetting that despite the fact that I am a human, I grew up with the things that you have taught me since I was a little boy', I argued.

Rasirine thought for a moment and said, 'The "normal time-reversal symmetry" is the movement through the magnetic fields running twice back and forth in time.'

I was still confused and asked, 'How does this happen? Pardon my ignorance, Ras, but I still do not understand'.

Rasirine continued in frustration. 'I told you, David, that it is difficult to understand, but you insist. For many years, your scientists wished to attain this kind of understanding. By breaking down time, moving through the magnetic fields makes things look the same'.

'Honestly, Ras, how can this movement break time down to make things look the same?'

Rasirine was exasperated and just said, 'It is exactly what was happening to you before when you said that you were spinning and you felt like you were everywhere and it felt like you were crossing the Atlantic Ocean in stormy weather'.

I did not want to tell Rasirine, but I was definitely lost trying to get my head around this 'normal time-reversal symmetry', which was bringing us back to our original state.

Planets were floating all around me spinning so slowly. Colours were flashing through my eyes, and suddenly I reached a halt. I stopped moving, and everything froze. I saw my life play through, and I heard a large voice behind me, around me. The voice seemed to be coming from everywhere. I was wondering, was this now 'normal time-reversal symmetry' or 'double time-reversal symmetry'?

I sort of understood that in the 'double time-reversal symmetry', it meant that the Neekans reversed time four times to get back things to their original state, and that in the 'normal time-reversal symmetry', they were reversing time twice to get things back to their original state. What I could not understand was how the Neekans knew when to apply each time reversal and bring things back to their original state at their wish and call.

'David Christopher Alexander Matthew Robert Harrison.' The voice stopped and took a large breath.

'He lies here with us today', another voice said, but this time, it was a female voice.

'David, wake up!' persisted the voice.

'Wake up, can you hear me!'

I tried to call out, but I could not. I could not do anything. I was stuck. I was sleeping but had a feeling of being awake. My heart wanted to call out, but I was frozen in the darkness. I could not see my arms or legs. I did not even feel like I had a body, as if my consciousness was floating through space with no one to accompany it on such a tiresome and long journey.

How did I know that my journey was going to be long? I thought. Then another question came to my mind: *How did I know I was not real? How am I in a position to even think? Do penguins have knees?* I thought. I trailed off through space, observing the different planets attempting to swim and forgetting about all my pointless questions and the stray voices here and there dominating my mind.

'I will send him to Tarnak', the woman's voice said.

I knew the name Tarnak; it sounded oddly familiar.

Yes! I thought. Penguins do have knees! In the last edition of *Science Magz*, I read it, and I can now see the whole article right before my eyes. However, the voices kept entering and leaving my mind whilst I continued to go on a hazy drift. I had no conception of time. It felt like I was drifting in a timeless vacuum that was euphoric.

At times, I was a little child brushing my hair and playing with my toys and Mum. Then I was in an adult state where I was thinking of my daughter and my wife Ras. I moved from the euphoric state from being a child to the adult state where my heart was feeling pain and suffering. I was terribly missing my family and especially my little girl, Lunette. I could not breathe or think. I wanted to get out. I wanted to see my child, my little girl. I wanted to see Rasirine. I could not stand being away from them!

'Daddy! Daddy!' My eyes jolted open with a force so great it almost knocked Lunette over.

I gasped for air. The air I had not had in my lungs for what had felt like years. Tarnak was standing over me, his eyes filled with joy that I had never seen before.

'You are back with us, son!' Tarnak cried out happily.

'Calypso! David is back! We have brought him back!' Tarnak called out.

Calypso came running in with a wide smile that could have probably sunk the *Titanic*. Although that shipwreck was an old historical fact, as a joke, it was no longer funny.

'How was it, David?' Calypso's warm and soothing voice asked me.

'How was what?' I asked, still readjusting to my lungs and brain and blood flow. I wanted a minute or two to concentrate and get my thoughts together in logical order so to be able to speak clearly and meaningfully.

'Oh, do not be shy, David. You are such a confident man. You know exactly where you were and how you feel, so tell me. The reason I am asking you is because if you provide me the information, I will be able to help you in a much more effective way. So if there is need next time, you won't have to go through the same process.'

I trusted Calypso, so I said, 'It was strange. I was floating, and I could not see my body. In my mind, I could hear snippets of conversations, and I constantly saw myself wearing Lunette's clothing and playing with dolls'. I recalled my state of darkness as if it were some mysterious movie that I had just seen.

'Hmm! Yes, I understand what happened to you, David. You went through a twentieth-degree coma, which is quite uncommon for humans . . . ', she said as she was entering some information in the holo-screen.

'Actually, you are the first case. I never thought that I would live to see the day a human would get through a twentieth-degree coma!'

I was quite lost for words and confused. *What is a twentieth-degree coma?* I wondered. 'What exactly is that?' I asked Calypso.

Calypso smiled and explained, 'Well, as you can probably guess, it is the degree of the unconscious level that a human being can undergo. It is a state from which the human cannot awake but the body is still living'.

'Well, good I understand that but, why twentieth degree? What does that mean?' I questioned.

'A twentieth-degree coma is when you are in a state of death and only the soul commands your emotions', Calypso replied.

'How?' I gasped.

'Mrs. Calypso, how is it possible that my emotional conscience stayed alive when my body and mind were basically dead?'

'David, you said so yourself. You said that you heard Lunette's voice, did you not?' Calypso demanded.

'Yes, something like that . . .'

'David, you may address me with my name, Calypso, or if you wish, you may call me Mother, like my daughter Rasirine. After all, I regard you as my son', Calypso suggested.

I took her advice and said, 'Mother, I really do not know what is happening lately with my mind. Firstly, I hear Sofron in my head all the time, and that was also during the Turquoise War and when I sleep. Sofron's voice was resonating in my head almost wherever I was. At times, I was able to block him out. Then the second voice that was pleasantly dominating my mind with sweetness was Lunette's voice'.

Calypso exclaimed, 'You are learning the Neekan's techniques, David!' She gave a hug and called Lunette and Tarnak inside the room. I really liked being in that room because it was painted with a ruby red colour and embellished with golden furniture with red and white curtains. Funny, I thought, we do not particularly need curtains if we are in space. However, Calypso made sure to make me feel that I was always at home.'

Then little Lunette said, 'Yes, Daddy, we do need the curtains in the spaceship especially if we are travelling near a sun!' Lunette giggled.

I was surprised again and asked Lunette, 'How did you know that I was thinking about the curtains, princess?'

'I can read your mind, Daddy.' Lunette said playfully.

'Lunti! Come here, princess.' I called out to her, and when she came close enough, I tickled her.

'Daddy, how come you call me Lunti . . . that is . . .'

'I know all about it, sweetheart, Mr. Fish told me about your little nickname games.'

Tarnak and Calypso chuckled and laughed whilst standing next to me, watching Lunette.

'Here comes the famous Mr. Fish!' Tarnak exclaimed with joy and laughter in his voice.

'Oh, sir! Mr. David, sir! Hello! Oh, I missed you! Oh hello! How is Mrs. Rasirine? You look good, sir, and your wounds are gone!'

I picked up the little gerbil and cuddled him. He rolled around in my palm and squeaked with delight. Lunette was also excited to see Mr. Fish.

'I missed you too, Mr. Fish, how did you know I would be back again and alive, hmm?' I asked him.

'I know a lot of things, sir! Not as much as you though', he squeaked happily and waddled off to be with his little friend Lunette.

'Hello, Mr. Fish! How have you been all this time away from me?' Lunette asked Mr. Fish.

'Well, Lunti, I was kind of feeling very lonely without your company, and I wanted some company too, so I have brought with me Molistora, and I would like you to meet her', whispered Mr. Fish.

'Molistora? I know her, is she your girlfriend, Mr. Fish?' Lunette eagerly asked.

Mr. Fish replied, 'Yes! You are correct, Lunti. I am going straight away to bring her here.'

I gave Lunette a ruffle in her hair and said, 'Off you go, Lunette, go play with Mr. Fish and Molistora'.

Lunette ran inside and jumped on my bed, holding Molistora and Mr. Fish.

Then Tarnak said, 'David, the time has come that you should now return back to your place. You will remember this as a dream, but when you wake up, we shall tell you all again. If you do not remember anything, do not worry because we will remind you, and so will your daughter.'

CHAPTER 31

I woke up in Rasirine's caring arms. She looked over at Glaron and smiled. Her eyes filled with tears. She screamed with joy. 'He is awake, Glaron! Oh, David! I am so happy you are back here with us. Lunette is safe too. She was with us here for quite some time, but do not worry she came. Glaron teleported her back to Orchadia to see you, and she will stay there.'

Glaron came towards my bed and greeted me. 'Hello, Chief Commander. How are you doing?'

'I am well, Glaron. It felt like I was dreaming all this time', I said in an exhausted voice. Even though I was revived, I still had pain all over my body, and I was on the verge of crying.

Rasirine asked me, 'Do you want to eat something? Are you hungry?'

'No, I am not hungry, Ras but can you tell me, where was I?' I asked.

'David, oh well, listen. Something is happening and I have to go. You stay here and do not move, OK? Bye, see you soon. I love you.'

I did not understand what Ras was saying. What was she going on about? My head was heavy, and I had a headache. I drank some water from the glass that was left near my tableside. I sat up and tried to reflect about all the events that I had gone through all the past years. Rasirine was back within a few minutes. I wanted to go out but, she said, 'David, you are not yet strong enough to join the war. You have been here for four nights only, and I am not going to let you go back out there.'

I started getting glimpses of the Turquoise War and the destruction caused in the city. 'I caused this disaster, Ras. I did this to the world. Let me get out of the tent and see the shame I have brought to your race.' I looked at her with hurt and disgust building inside me.

I had brought innocent men and women to fight in a war that was unnecessary to be fought.

'What shame are you talking about, David!?' Rasirine asked.

'The destruction of the city Ras, this is what is a shame. It was not really necessary.' I responded unhappily.

'It is not a shame! You have won! You have saved the Neekans from further captivity and slavery that humans have put us through! Do you know that in another seventeen countries of your earth slavery still exists among your human fellow beings? You have nothing to be ashamed of!'

I sat motionless and studied Rasirine's face for a few seconds before I asked her 'You healed all those men, children and women next to us did you not?'

Rasirine did not say anything but simply nodded her head in agreement. I got up and glanced on my teleport the state of the city.

'Look at what I have made the Neekans do! What I made my daughter witness here in this battlefield! Is that saving you? Is that deserving of pride!? It is a plague on my mind to think we have won! We have not! This city is under constant surveillance by countries all over the globe Rasirine.' I wanted to be left alone so I shot Rasirine a look that signaled my wish. Rasirine understood and left without saying a word. I was sitting here, in the tent, pondering about all the disaster that had occurred all around me. I stood up and made an attempt to get out of the tent when Glaron's voice stopped me.

'Hey David, you better sit down you heard what Rasirine said!'

'Glaron let me ask you a question. Why did Rasirine not react to my statement about the international authorities keeping an eye on us?'

'David is it not obvious?'

I shook my head vigorously with disagreement. 'No, Glaron it really is not!'

He sighed 'When Rasirine took you in from the building you had collapsed, you were out cold. You had died. Not a single breath. Rasirine sent you to Orchadia for her parents to heal you whilst she continued the war here.'

'Do not tell me Glaron that Rasirine used the 'normal time-reversal symmetry' again?'

Glaron responded in the affirmative adding, 'Do not worry genocide was not Rasirine's intention, in each country we have disabled the main attackers from their weaponry. They are all living in a safe place with food and shelter but the condition was to pledge on their lives and on the lives of their families that they would never enslave us again. The majority of them are peaceful with no intention of war but a few others are not so and they threaten to kill us all.'

'Right, so basically what you are trying to tell me is that the Neekans have the humans in cages and are too weak to fight.'

'Quite right! I am glad you are catching up!'

'No, Glaron, this was not the plan because we are doing exactly what they did to the Neekans and this means that we are never going to finish this war. We are never going to foster peaceful coexistence between the Neekans and Humans. It will only promote further mass deaths until everyone loses and no one wins anything at the end.'

Glaron interrupted me, 'You were dead for a whole year and this prevented you from witnessing the atrocities that they committed against us.'

'This is exactly what I mean Glaron. We have to put a stop to all of this.'

Glaron became angry at me as if we were enemies now. I could not understand his conduct.

'Rasirine never gave up believing that I was going to return, did she Glaron?'

'What?' Glaron responded angrily.

'Rasirine did not give up on me coming back did she?'

'No, she was convinced that you would be healed. This is why she teleported you immediately to Tarnak so that you would be healed.'

'You are angry that I am back, Glaron because you have always wanted Rasirine for yourself. You hated the fact that she chose me over you and that even for a whole year she fought in my place because she knew I would be able to come back. You hated the fact that she did not love you? Is that right?'

Glaron's face turned red. 'It is not fair! What have you done David to deserve the daughter of Tarnak? You have caused a war that she had to fight in. I would have never done that. I would have protected her from all this menacing events. You did nothing all this time and you have not even found the book. What is so good about you?'

I looked at him plainly and said 'that is where you are wrong my friend. I may have not found the book but I know where to find it. Further, it was not me who caused this war. The Turquoise War was initiated by the Neekans for their freedom which I believed in and still believe in for any living creature.'

Glaron stared at me with anger in his eyes and barked his reply, 'You did everything with Tarnak's help and Rasirine's love. You did absolutely nothing for the Neekans.'

Tarnak beamed himself beside me.

'Glaron, you called my name? What service do you ask of me now?'

'Hello Tarnak. My apologies I have not called you for anything I am very sorry for calling out your name so loudly. It is just that David and

I are having a very heated discussion.' Glaron attempted to cover up his anger and false accusations towards me.

Tarnak was straight forward and said to Glaron, 'Oh, but do I have the impression that it is something, along the lines that you doubt that David has found the book? You feel as though he has done nothing towards this Turquoise War but sleeping peacefully, whilst he sacrificed his people to save us and fought next to my daughter, do you not?'

'Yes, as a matter of fact I do think so.'

'Glaron you have been wronged in your life but that does not mean that one must go against his closest friend. David knows where the book is and if he finds it he will be able to save the collapse of the universe.'

Glaron was not at all satisfied with Tarnak's answer and asked, 'How do we know that the universe is collapsing? Orchadia is not yet burning.'

'Look at the anachronisms child. Swords and crossbows amongst laser guns and beam rays, radios functioning back and record keeping amongst holo-transfer. Look around you! Where are you sleeping? In tents! Time is collapsing around itself and every day that passes it comes nearer.'

'You are just protecting David Tarnak and you see him in a more favourable light than me.'

With a more austere tone of voice Tarnak said, 'That is enough Glaron! You are not to come here again. I will send you back to Orchadia so that you can join your family and remain there with them in safety. You may say 'Good bye' to David now, because I will be teleporting you shortly in Orchadia.'

Glaron's face lost colour, from a turquoise he became white, whiter than a sheet. He stood tall, said nothing to Tarnak but he said 'Good bye' to me and then left the tent.

Tarnak turned to me, 'I will find Rasirine and instruct her to join you immediately because you must leave tonight. The book must be found before dawn Earth time. You have thirty-five days left for Orchadian time. Do you know where it is?'

I responded with hesitation, 'Not precisely but I recall that Sofron had mentioned something about the book that it never existed. I know now, that it was a trick of his to dissuade me from pursuing the search of the book so that he can find it before anyone else.'

Tarnak replied, 'David my boy, the only help that I can assist you with is to inform you that the book is said to be buried by the Neekan elders deep within the sands of Earth.'

'I have a faint idea Tarnak where the book may have been buried by your elders. I have in mind a place that is of great historical value for humans and it will still be in future. I will find it. I give you my word.'

Tarnak said his last few words before disappearing from the tent, 'I know you will find it and you know how important it is that you do find it.'

CHAPTER 32

Rasirine and I set out on the quest for *The Secrets of Orchadia* as I had promised Tarnak.

I just remembered and asked Rasirine, 'Did you leave them the decree?'

'Yes, David, I did.'

'Did you mention in the decree that my main order is to cease war and killing one another? Instead they should show compassion, understanding, and love for one another?'

'Yes, I have made sure that they would also spread the word of love, peace, and compassion for humans. David, please, I am tired, we have been walking through the desert for hours. The book could be anywhere.'

'Then it is our job to find the book. After all, I promised your father. I will commence searching, and you should remain here and be on the lookout for anything strange occurring.'

Rasirine pointed to a llama in the distance, which she found to be entertaining for its appearance.

I was quite annoyed with Rasirine as she seemed not to take this search seriously. Probably it was a Neekan way of not getting all uptight about quests, and I said, 'Right, other than laughing at certain comical anachronisms, look at the detail, Ras.'

'What do you mean, David?'

'For example, if you see any strange encryptions or a strange scene, then tell me.'

'I do not think there are any strange scenes, David.'

'Oh! Look down all around us. What do you see, Ras?'

Rasirine seemed even more disinterested since she was exhausted from walking in this endless desert and responded, 'I do not know what you are talking about! All I can see around us is that there is sand everywhere and no pyramids anymore. All the pyramids have turned to dust'.

'Except that llama . . .'

'What?' She paused and rolled her eyes. 'The llama is not a pyramid, David. Are you delusional? Has the extreme heat of the desert affected you?'

'No, Ras, I thought that the llama might be a clue for us to locate the book.'

'We really cannot use a llama as a guide. Honestly, David, is there anything else we could go by?'

'Of course, your father had told us that *The Secrets of Orchadia* lie buried deep beneath the greatest sands of the human's terrestrial globe, Earth, and it is kept hidden for centuries amongst the common things! It must be here, the greatest sands! Egypt, pyramids, secrets, and its people all turned to dust over the centuries. The numerous wars have destroyed civilizations time after time, and so many things have been buried in the sands deeper and deeper into the Earth. Why would it not be here?'

'This is too easy of a location for a book to be hidden by the Neekans, David', Rasirine said.

'What?' I responded as I had thought it to be a very clever and ingenious deduction for a clue.

Rasirine insisted, 'It is much too easy to be Egypt! Sand—it could be everywhere as in sandstones, sediments, in oceans, and anywhere else that there is sand in any kind and form on this planet. Egypt is much too easy of a place to hide a book'.

'Well, where do you suggest the book might be, Ras?' I asked disappointedly.

'Perhaps you are right, David, and I am taking back what I said before. This place might be the right spot to look for the book!'

My face lightened up with glee and said to Rasirine, 'Right, then let's get cracking'.

We set up camp under a lonely tree and searched around for any details the normal eye could miss.

'It is just sand from here to the end of the horizon. Animals have not been seen here for centuries, and no one bothers to come here anymore. Everyone has now moved to other galaxies. There is better climate over there. The ones who lived here now live in the cities. This place is just a big wasteland.'

'I know, Ras, but we cannot lose hope now! We have got to find the book.'

'David! Come and have a look here!' Rasirine called out.

I quickly ran to see Rasirine's discovery. 'Look at what I have found! Look at the markings on it. It looks like an Orchadian symbol, but I do not know exactly what it means.'

I jumped around on the spot and remarked to Rasirine, 'This is the language of your people, which means that you have been here many centuries ago. Contact Tarnak and send him a photo through contactogram'.

'Should I contact my father? I think that my father is not supposed to help us, David! If my father helps us, then the mission is aborted because it will ruin the code. If the code is ruined, then the dream with the book will disappear. This is our first challenge, and we must get through it on our own!'

After hours of hard thinking and comparing the mark to thousands of ancient alphabets, Rasirine thought of a clue. 'David! Ancient Noxas Orchadian! You were right, I should have known!'

'Aha! Bravo! Let's see what we can find.'

'This shape represents the letter *F* and this one the letter *R*, the next one *A*, and the next *N, C, E*. The word is "France"! Oh! I have always wanted to go to France! But why would the Neekan elders put directions to get to France in Egypt?'

We spun so quickly, nausea was quickly rising in me with the time travel pod.

'Get up, Ras! Let's go find the next clue!' I said as I stood up from our recent time travel spin through the fabric of space and reaching France.

'We are in France! But wait, we are not in Paris!' Rasirine said, indicating that she was disappointed.

'Do not worry, Ras I will take you to Paris as soon as this is all over. Thirty-three days left. Use the holo-pad to find out the exact location. Do not forget to also send a copy to Tarnak and send Lunette my love.'

'Wait a minute, I am trying to do a hundred things at once, give me a second please', Rasirine complained, and then she teleported us to southeast of France.

'Right, we are in southeast France, Marseille. This is quite a big town, but hang on, where are all the people?' Rasirine asked.

'The town was plagued with cancerous substances, and most of the humans developed severe forms of cancer. But thanks to a new DNA scientific development, they are on their way to recovery. They have the best treatment. They have plenty of nutritious food and fresh water. They will have no health issues any longer.'

We walked past the abandoned city. Our only company was the sun moving gracefully across the sky, shining on to the coastal land.

After walking along the beach for hours, Rasirine asked if we could stop because she was detecting a sound from her holo-pad.

I dug and dug until I had dug about ten meters down in the ground.

Rasirine was getting tired and said, 'David, stop. This is pointless'.

'No, Ras, we are just about to get the book. I remember a very popular saying that we humans have: "A winner never quits and a quitter never gets to enjoy the rewards!" Let me find the next rock!'

Then I hit something metallic; it was a large metal case.

'I told you, Ras!'

Rasirine was even more excited than me. 'Bring it up! Bring it up, and let's open it!'

I lifted up the heavy case that was only about thirty centimeters long but weighed more than fifteen kilograms. 'Boy, is this one heavy!' I exclaimed. 'Oh! Do you think we found a treasure instead of the book?' I asked Rasirine.

Rasirine was not as well informed about the pirates raiding the seas despite the some reading she had done on the subject, and she said, 'I have read about your pirates in my history classes! They used to put all their stolen treasure in a chest and then go dig a hole and bury it!'

I shook my head in disagreement. 'Remind me to teach you some facts about human history relating to pirates because what you have just said is not what the pirates were doing!'

I pulled up the chest and placed it next to me. On the chest there was a complex symbolic password locking the chest and then long rows of characters and symbols. Rasirine came and sat next to me and said that the symbol represented a combination code that she could read in the Orchadian language.'

'Read the code to me, Ras. I would like to know what it says.'

Rasirine said, 'David, it is not just a code, it has also a message for you.'

I looked at Rasirine, puzzled, 'How did they know of me, Ras?'

'Oh, do not be so frightened, David. Are you forgetting that you are the boy who was chosen to save the universe?'

'No, Ras, I am not forgetting it, but what I am asking is *how* did they know that I were to be the one to save the universe?'

Rasirine tried to make things easier for me and said, 'You did not think they would know your name, right? Well, do not be afraid. The Neekans knew exactly that it was you, the boy with the name David, who would come here and find it. You are Sofron's son. Remember, Sofron was with the Neekans for many years'.

'Yes, but I do not consider Sofron as my father.'

Rasirine continued, 'Now let me read the message and probably you will be able to understand'.

> *Dear David,*
>
> *We have placed the book in a very secure place and it may be life threatening for you and Rasirine. You must follow exactly all instructions otherwise you will be risking your life. In order to unlock the secret combination you must enter what two things are most important to Orchadians. Rasirine will be with you and she will be of assistance to you but it is you who should enter the secret code. Good luck to you and Rasirine.*

'Well, that is not frightening at all!' I said and started thinking about the two values that the Orchadians cherish most. 'Hmm, Ras, what do you think if I say that the Neekans cherish *honesty* and *valor* the most?'

'No! I am afraid that you are incorrect, David.'

What could they be? I thought. I stood up to think and paced up and down along the beach. I saw some starfish on the edge, and I picked them up and threw them back into the ocean where they belonged. Some fish came up near my feet and then swam back vigorously into the deep water. Then I thought, probably it was *love* and *amenability*.

The more I thought about it, the more I was convinced that this may have been the answer, and I called out to Rasirine, 'Rasirine! I think I have the answer'.

I walked towards her from the edge of the water. My pants wet from the ocean waves clashing to my knees, and my feet were covered in sand. I could almost see her hair in the fading sunlight as she awoke from her slumber.

'Ras, I have got it!'

Rasirine smiled and giggled. 'All right, genius, what is it the answer?'

'Well, the two values that the Neekans value and pride themselves with are *love* and *amenability*!'

She got up and hugged me. 'You got it! I am so proud of you! Let's see what the casing has inside quickly!' and pulled me by my hand towards the casing.

I typed in the initial letters of the two words L and A. The answer was correct. Rasirine said that now we were heading to America because L and A stand also for Los Angeles.

Rasirine and I exchanged happy looks as the casing opened slowly. A little note was cradled under what looked like a canister of toothpaste, binoculars, and two high-pressure laser guns capable of burning someone's heart within seconds.

Rasirine got too excited with the guns and the toothpaste. 'Oh! This is a sub-atomic shrinking paste! This will come in handy if we have got to get out of a sticky situation!'

Then Rasirine said, 'These three items should be very useful in America, especially if you come across any difficult circumstances.'

'I am so glad you have found the next clue, David, but be prepared to face more challenging situations ahead of our journey. My people know the future,' she said sadly.

I responded to Rasirine, 'Well, my love, if something happens to me, you will have to continue without me to save the universe and become queen of Orchadia with whomever you choose as your king. I am sure and you will raise Lunette well'.

Rasirine got very angry with me. She approached and slapped me across the face.

'What was that for, Ras!?' I asked her.

'The slap was to see if I can build some sense in you. Listen to me well and stop uttering stupidities. You are not going anywhere, and I am not becoming queen without you!' she said with anger still drawn in her face.

CHAPTER 33

I went into the tent to gather our staff, and then when I got out, I saw Rasirine pointing a gun towards me. And in a deep voice, she said, 'I have told you that I will win next time'.

Sofron once more was making my mission impossible. He had transformed himself into Rasirine so as to trick me. I stood tall up against him and asked, 'Where have you taken Rasirine? What have you done with her this time again? Why do you keep doing this? I have proven to you that wherever you take her, I will always find her. There is no way you will ever win.'

'Oh really?' Sofron, the one and only evil master of the universe who had shaped himself into being Rasirine so as to conquer me, responded.

'You deceitful creature! Where have you taken Rasirine? What have you done with her?'

Sofron replied sarcastically, 'She went fishing, and one can assume that she has drowned in the deep waters of the ocean'.

My body froze for a moment, but I still had some courage to ask him, 'You killed her?'

Then I became angry and charged towards him. 'You killed my Rasirine!?'

Then Sofron changed back to his normal, usual appearance.

'What is it that you want from me? Why do you want to take everything I love? How could you kill the woman I love so much?'

'I do not know. Do not ask me stupid questions. I just wanted to immobilize you emotionally so that I could gain control of the universe without you bothering me all the time. Well, I suppose now that Rasirine is dead, you have no hope of saving the universe.'

'You are bluffing,' I responded.

'Why do you always think that you know everything? You are just like your mother, you think you are all smart and intelligent, but you are really not!' His voice became uneasy and unsteady.

'Let me tell you this, Sofron. I know that Rasirine is alive, and no matter what you do, you will never stop me from accomplishing my mission.'

Sofron tried to interrupt by approaching closer to me, pointing a gun towards my chest with hatred and a sense of defeat. I was not at all afraid. I had to say what I had to say and I pressed on. 'You might think that you still have some love for me, but deep down, you know what, I am not at all interested in you.'

'Why do you fight me, David? I am your father, and I only want us to be a team.'

'Nothing you say or do will change my opinion about you. The only last thing that I request of you is to bring back Rasirine. I swear, Sofron, if you do not bring back Rasirine sound and safe, you will lose.'

Sofron's face turned red, and he insisted in his tactics. 'You have no weapons to fight me. How will you? I will not release Rasirine, and I will make sure that she will suffer with me for eternity.'

Suddenly, a terrible headache erupted in my mind. I fell to the ground writhing with pain. 'Do not listen to what he says, David!' It was Rasirine's voice warning me. I then opened my eyes and saw Rasirine standing in front of me. 'Ras! You are safe!'

Sofron was alarmed and said, 'She is contacting you!? I do not understand how is she able to do that? I have disabled all communication and changed the wiring. Everything she ever was has been deleted, how could she have survived this?'

Sofron decided to walk backwards and scan the area with his eyes to see if this was some optical illusion.

Rasirine called out to me. 'I do not have long to go, David, but listen to me. You must save the book. I will access your memory, and you will never remember me. Please go on and save Orchadia'. I saw her standing there with tears flooding her eyes, gulping at every word. 'I will always love you. Stay strong. Fight for me and fight for Lunette' were Rasirine's last words.

My head was about to explode with pain. I was screaming from the excruciating pain. 'No, Rasirine! Please do not go. I do not want to forget you. I will be half the man if you are not here with me.' I fisted my hands down hard on to the sand, and tears ran from my eyes. I was screaming, and my heart felt like it was about to self-destruct. My head felt like a chunk of it had been removed and thrown away.

'Sofron, hand me back my things', I stood up and spoke to Sofron.

'Why did you throw me on the ground? That is a bit low, is it not?' I asked him.

Sofron was standing there with awe and asked, 'Are you not upset about Rasirine?' I looked at him blankly.

'Who is Rasirine? Stop with your gibber and return my things immediately', I said, annoyed this time with Sofron.

Sofron dropped his weapons and looked at me and said, 'I stole your wife, I hid her and I killed her . . . do you not remember?'

'I do not have a wife!' I argued.

'Now go back where you came from, all right!' Sofron stood up at tried to walk away. I took the gun and shot him in the heart.

'Ah! You sly boy, but by now, you should know that when you kill me, I will and do come back.'

'No, you will not this time, Sofron. I too have done my research. Where have you hidden the girl you mentioned?'

'Who are you talking about? Rasirine? The one who was going to help you save the universe right? Well, I have told you that she is dead. You cannot do anything.'

My head was throbbing as if someone was trying to tell me something, but nothing was coming through.

'I have no wife!' I yelled at Sofron and then shot him repetitively in the heart and then knelt down beside him. I checked his pulse, and after a few minutes, I came to the conclusion that he was dead.

Next stop LA in America. I have twenty-nine days left to save the world all on my own.

CHAPTER 34

'Daddy... Daddy... please remember Mummy...'

'Who is it? Who said that!?' I demanded as I was turning around in circles to check my surroundings.

The pain pounded my head again; snippets of a child dying in my arms, calling out to me, appeared in my mind. Pictures flew across my eyes, and memories started to spill in piece by piece. Who was this child? I thought. I shook the thought out of my head.

'Daddy... save Mummy...', the same voice could be heard haunting me.

'Aaaaaah!' I yelled as I collapsed to the ground.

A projection of an image of a little girl was now in front of my eyes.

'Who are you!?' I called out to the child.

The little girl started crying and calling me, 'Daddy, Daddy! It is me! Lunette! How could you not remember me?'

'I do not know who you are. I do not know who I am or what I am. Why am I here? What am I doing?'

A strange blue man came into the scene and kept saying, 'Memories momentum, memories momentum.' Then he said, 'David, I am your father-in-law. In a few moments, you will start remembering things and what your mission is. You have been fighting in the Turquoise War with my daughter, Rasirine, who is also your spouse, and you have a little girl together.'

An unbearable pain shook my mind. I felt dizzy, and my mind was spinning. I fell into the trench that was besides the silver casing. I tried to get back up, but I could not, despite my efforts to climb up by clenching on the sides of the wall.

One by one, the memories of various events were constantly unfolding before my sight, which made my brain spin even more. I was not able to keep track of them. I was not even able to put together a logical sequence.

I lost faith in my thinking process, and I called for Tarnak. 'Tarnak, I remember Rasirine, but what happened to her? Where is she?'

Tarnak's face became stern and unkind. 'You will not find Rasirine. I will not allow you to because she has betrayed you by removing your past memories. How are you going to fight?'

'Tarnak, do not be harsh with Rasirine, she only tried to conceal my emotions for her in order to keep on fighting. Please let me find her. I cannot and will not find the book of Orchadia without her.'

'OK, David, I will let you find Rasirine, but it is only for Lunette's sake.'

I was extremely happy for Tarnak's decision, and I called out to see Lunette. 'Lunette, come forward, sweetheart, Daddy wants to see you before the screen switches off!'

Lunette came running to the screen, 'Daddy! You remembered me!'

'Of course I did, princess! I am going to find Mummy too, and we will soon be home, I love you very much. I have got to go now. I will speak to you soon! Love you!'

'Love you too, Daddy!' she said, giggling off.

I caught Tarnak off guard whilst he was smiling at Lunette, and I quickly reminded him, 'What did you say sir, for Lunette?'

He humbly nodded and repeated, 'Only for Lunette'.

CHAPTER 35

In Portugal! How did Sofron send Rasirine there? I thought to myself as I was tracking down Rasirine's current geographical position through the portal pod. I was ready to go and meet Rasirine. I used the portal pod and sent myself to the exact location where she was sent.

'David, you have found me', she said wearily.

'Rasirine, oh my sweetheart, how are you? What has Sofron done to you?!'

Sofron had Rasirine cuffed to the wall by her wrists. Rasirine looked even thinner than before. Sofron had not fed her for four days and had not given her any water for hours.

I took out my water bottle and gave her some to drink slowly. Then I took care of her wrists until she was able to use her Neekan powers to heal her wounds.

'What about Sofron? He will definitely be back. We take one step forward, and he comes out of nowhere and pulls us ten steps back', Rasirine said in an exasperated tone. 'I am tired of fighting him.'

With an air of relief, I tried to pacify Rasirine by telling her, 'Sofron is dead!'

'This is what you said last time too, David, but he kept reappearing.'

'I know, Rasirine, but this time, I have given him a placebo for his regeneration, which will not work. I am serious! I told him that his whole renewal was a trick of the mind. I have deleted his renewal, so Sofron is actually dead. I measured him for an hour, and no signs of life returned to the monitor!'

Rasirine could not believe it and asked me again so that I could reassure her. 'You did it? You have defeated the evil master of the universe?'

I stood tall and proudly replied, 'Yes! Yes, yes, I did it, Ras!'

I helped Rasirine stand up from the ground. She was feeble and weak. I took out the medicine I had brought with me from Orchadia and gave her some to drink. She was not well enough to travel to America.

We walked through the deserted city and decided to set up camp on the borders when a little girl appeared and invited us to follow her to her home. Rasirine and I politely refused the invitation. Then the same little girl turned into a large insect-like creature with orange-and-pink antennae.

'I am Foneya, queen of the Wassmar conglomeration. You are new to this land. You shall be eaten. You have five minutes to come. Otherwise, we shall collect you ourselves.' Then she transformed back to the little girl that she was before.

Rasirine got into her warrior's mode and replied 'Oh no! We will not follow you.'

Rasirine pulled out the laser beam guns from my pocket and threw me one, crying out, 'Shoot what you see, and shoot what you don't!'

Rasirine shot the little girl. The little girl flickered between her alien and human form and finally died in her carnivorous insect form. Then instantly, there was a storm of other insects flying towards us, but they did not attack us. Just one of the carnivorous insects stood apart from the rest and said, 'We have been waiting for you, David. We are acting upon Sofron's instructions to kill you.'

'Before you kill me, may I ask you please to tell me which planet are you from and why do you utter such phrases filled with verbal stream of venom?'

The carnivorous insects did not reply but instead they came closer, and in a threatening manner, they were baring their sharp pincers and fangs.

One of the ugly-looking insects came towards Rasirine and me and pointed its machine straight at us. The strange machine released some bleeping sounds and then said, 'Test detected—life form is not human'.

Rasirine and I exchanged looks of surprise, but we did not have time to waste, and she immediately aimed at the insects.

I yelled out, 'Shoot them, Ras! Just shoot!' and I started shooting at the insects too.

We were firing the laser beams one after another, and the insects' bodies were sizzling and falling to the ground, releasing groans and alien noises accompanied with deep whizzing. We kept shooting at the insects till there was not a single alien standing.

'Can we just go back to Orchadia?' I asked as I was exhausted from this ugly encounter.

'Yes, sure you are right, David. We are better off going back to Orchadia. I think we will rest better there', Rasirine replied. 'Got everything ready, David, for our teleporting?' she asked me with a large smile.

'Yes, I have got everything ready, let's go', I replied and then noticed her lip was burst open.

'Your lips are bleeding. Did one of the alien insects attack you?'

'Yes, David whilst I was shooting them, one approached me very close at an arm's distance, and hit me on the lips with its leg. They are called Wassmars. Do not be concerned. I am fine, no need to worry about me. I am fine', she said, a little annoyed.

'I am sorry, I care about you', I mumbled.

'I know you care about me, but you care too much about me, and this is the reason why I wiped your memory—'

I quickly interrupted her, 'I am not having this conversation, Ras. Love is in the air!'

'That human statement is false. The air contains oxygen, nitrogen, and carbon dioxide for your information, David.'

'Did you contact your father, Ras, to tell him that we are on our way?'

'No, I have not because I thought I would surprise him with a little knock-knock on the door', and she gave me a little nod.

I pressed the button, and we whizzed through space and safely landed back into Orchadia in the main hall of Tarnak's palace.

'Oh! What a surprise? David and Rasirine are back!' Tarnak said excitingly.

'Welcome back, my children!' Calypso cheered.

Then it was Lunette's turn. She did not seem to be as excited. 'We have got to talk!'

CHAPTER 36

'What is the matter, Lunette?' Rasirine asked while picking her up.

'Mr. Fish said that he does not like his girlfriend anymore, and may I ask what took you so long to return?'

Rasirine smiled and said, 'I am sure Mr. Fish will be fine, and as for delaying our return back to Orchadia, the reason is that we could not find our way back. We got lost in some countries on planet Earth.'

I quickly added, in order to avoid any disappointment for our imminent departure again since our stay was going to be short, 'Lunette, Mummy and I may have to leave again pretty soon, but we will definitely come back.'

Lunette smiled and waved us off along with Tarnak and Calypso.

Destination was keyed in. 'One thousand and twenty four Sofa Street and Ron Street, Los Angeles'

'Does not that sound a little . . . suspicious?' Rasirine remarked.

'Why would it be suspicious, Ras?' I asked with curiosity, thinking what this new challenge awaiting for us to tackle is.

Rasirine insisted, 'Read the two names of the streets together, David, don't they sound like Sofron's name? They clearly say Sofron?'

'Well, the next clue cannot wait forever. Time is ticking away, and we need to get there as soon as possible! We will take on whatever is on our way. Do not lose courage', I said to Rasirine, trying to dissuade her mind from allowing any negative thoughts entering it.

When we arrived at our destination, we looked around with disbelief. The location was an old, disheveled home with a big sign on the main entrance with two words 'Keep out'. Rasirine looked at me as if there was definitely something wrong with the instructions.

'Oh! An old home! Let's go inside and see what we can find, Ras!'

Rasirine gave me a strange look and said, 'Yes, David, let us enter the deserted house. I am curious too to find out what is in there, but we have to be very careful.'

Curiosity rose up inside me like a boiling pot of water, and I called out to Rasirine, 'Come on, Ras, hurry up! Stop checking the house on the outside. We have no time!' And I ran into the home as Rasirine was still checking the surroundings of the house.

'David, wait! I do not think it is safe to enter the house!' Rasirine called out in frustration, but it was too late because I had already gone inside.

The old door made a very loud creak as I opened it wide enough for me to enter the room, and the floorboards creaked at every single step I was taking. It was creepy and scary walking through this deserted home. For a moment, I thought that it would be wise to check for some more clues from the chest.

I opened the chest, and I found a note instructing me. 'Follow your instincts and you will find whatever you are looking for, only if you trust yourself.' I closed the chest, and I started thinking about the instructions. I then called out to Rasirine, who was now steps behind me, shining her torch at every sound.

'Are you afraid, Ras?' I asked, turning around suddenly.

I heard a little gasp as Rasirine reacted, and I tried to reassure her. 'Do not worry, Ras, nothing is going to hurt us', I said with a little too much confidence because as I turned back to walk farther down into the hallway, a large white creature appeared.

This white creature was so enormous in size that it had to crouch itself under its own body in order to fit in the confined space. It had a strange-looking skin, like scales, but it was injured because there was a stream of blood flowing from its stomach.

I did not want to go too close because its tentacles were spreading in an attempt to clutch on to me. It had four long arms with two tentacles on each arm. Its eyes were yellow with a dark circles reflecting the light from Rasirine's torch.

'Ras, do not come any closer and stop reflecting your torch. The beast is getting frustrated, turn back and run!' I screamed at Rasirine who shot it in the leg before she left the room, but we could not leave the house. We were both trapped.

'You really did not have to do that, Ras. Look now, we are stuck in a house with an angry gigantic beast half injured and probably hungry. I am sure we have aggravated it more with our recent break-in.'

'I suggest we leave right now, David, I am not sure if the book is located here', Rasirine said, uncharacteristically stressed.

'We cannot get out, we are trapped. We need to get another clue to free ourselves from this monstrous creature. Do not despair, Rasirine!?' I said with an assured and strong tone of voice.

The monstrous creature reacted to my comment as if it understood what I was saying to Ras. I stepped towards it, faced it, and greeted the beast. 'Hello, I am David', and I extended my hand out towards it. It made some strange alien noises, and it also extended its hand with its two tentacles and shook my hand vigorously.

'Do you speak English?' I asked the beast, which seemed to be kinder to us.

It shook its head uttering, 'Not well, I am injured', and it turned its head away, embarrassed.

'No, please do not be embarrassed. We do not want to hurt you and upset you in any way. My friend Rasirine was quite frightened and did not know how to react to your moans and groans.'

Rasirine plucked up some courage and asked the beast, 'Can you help us find the secret clue for our book *The Secrets of Orchadia*?'

'No, this I cannot help you with.'

It shook its head and then rested by unplugging one of its tentacles. Within seconds, it was releasing a sound like a deep snoring but at 200 decibels, which was absolutely deafening.

I heard a little voice in my head directing me to 'go left'.

I did not tell Rasirine but I said to her, 'I think we should go left, Ras'.

Rasirine did not object, and in very slow, soft steps, we managed to search the rooms on the left without disturbing the monstrous beast from its sleep. In the last room, I noticed a stray sock. Normally, I would consider such a piece of clothing as a trivial item not worthy of attention, but something about that sock intrigued me.

Rasirine looked at the sock and whispered, 'The sock is our next clue'.

'I was thinking the same thing too, Ras, that the sock is not here by chance.'

'It feels like there is something in the sock. I will go and have a look.'

I took a few more steps and picked it up. I put my hand around it and did not feel anything then I reached into the sock. It was huge! I pulled out a book and a fish tank, a ladder and a cat.

'How could everything fit into this sock? When I first held the sock in my hand, it felt empty', I told Rasirine, perplexed.

'It is the dimension change in space travelling', Rasirine was quick to answer my question.

'Look inside the sock, it indicates an opening in the floor! It looks like a door to the basement!' I pointed out to Rasirine.

'Yes, I think so too, and I can further see something else glowing down there. Let's enter the sock and have a closer look!'

I first wriggled into the sock and then Rasirine followed. We reached the front of a large basement underneath the floor of the disheveled house. The basement was very clean, and there was not even a single dust speck anywhere.

A strange voice spoke deeply, as if it was coming from a faraway place high up in a mountain. 'I have waited so many years for you, David. I know very well that you are the saviour of our universe. You have come in search of the book, have you not?' It was the same female voice that was haunting me in my dreams for years.

I was overtaken by my fear having to face the woman of my nightmares. I immediately regrouped and maintained an unshaken poise, managing to nod at the woman in an affirmative and then said, 'Yes'.

Rasirine was standing right beside me when I asked the woman, 'Madam, you are the woman who has been coming to my dreams ever since I was a child? Am I correct?'

'Yes, I am', she responded and continued. 'Do not be afraid because I am here to help you in the last leg of the journey to find the book.'

Rasirine squeezed my hand tightly and gave me a half smile as we were both waiting for the woman's advice to finally get to our destination in finding the book.

'The book is right here, David, in the golden case on your far right. The case is locked, and it will only open when you recite the words of the hope poem that I have asked you to memorise and remember. Do you recall my instructions, David?'

'Of course I do, madam. You were instructing me to recite it every single night during my childhood.'

Rasirine supported my response by adding, 'David used to tell me about it, madam, and he would recite the whole poem word for word without making any mistakes.'

'I am glad to hear so, Rasirine. Now you must proceed to the golden case and hold the lock in your hands, David, when you recite the poem of hope.'

Rasirine nudged me to recite the poem. 'Go on, recite the poem. This is the moment, David, the moment that you will unlock and find the hidden book, *The Secrets of Orchadia*, the book that will also save the universe.'

I did not miss the chance and started reciting the poem whilst holding the lock.

> The universe shall crash and burn,
> No one will fight,
> Or see their turn,
> Go on through the endless night,
> The secrets of Orchadia,
> Are the ones we should hold dear,
> For one will save Orchadia,
> When the time is near,
> The secrets shall protect us,
> And end the war we fear,
> The universe shall bow down,
> To the wisest of the Neekans,
> No one will ever cast a frown,
> Upon our great achievements

As I was holding the lock in my hands whilst I was reciting the poem, it started heating up, and a vibrant golden light shone through it.

Then the voice of the woman said, 'The secrets of Orchadia have been revealed to the saviour of the universe!'

This was the last we heard of the woman as she disappeared in the darkness. The book rose from the golden case into the air and then landed in my open hands.

Rasirine was emotionally touched by the whole process and was patently proud of my efforts, and a tear of happiness slid down her face from her expressive eyes.

'You found it, you found the book, David!' she said.

As I turned the first page, a note slipped out. I opened it and read it aloud so that Rasirine could hear too.

To my son, David,

David, you will be the one who will end the war I started between the Neekans and Humans. I always knew that you were stronger than me. Go on and save Orchadia and the universe.

Your father,
Sofron

I shut the book and took Rasirine by the hand and walked back upstairs. We said our goodbyes to the monster who was guarding the disheveled house and then walked out from the house to the open space. We walked until we reached a park where we sat down on the grass. I re-opened the book to the page that felt most comfortable. Then a heading caught my attention: 'The collapse of the universe, year 2573', by Lunette Harrison.

Dear Father,

You are probably sitting comfortably on the grass at the park with Mother, reading this section of the book. My duty is to inform both of you of what is going to happen. You must activate the five shifts in the fabric of the universe between Orchadia and Earth within three days of each. After this task is accomplished, you will have to detonate them all at the same exact time. Then the double-reversal time symmetry line will be activated to cause an explosion and return the whole universe to normality.

Rasirine was listening to the instructions as I was reading them loudly and said, 'Well, that sounds easy! We must get the shifts first!' And she quickly platted her long blue hair to keep it off her face.

'The first shift self-destructs in three hours. It is in Orchadia, in the Aprule region', I informed Rasirine when I consulted my teleport.

'That is my neighbouring hometown. Let's go!' she said.

We ran from shift to shift, crossing the Arctic plains, deserts, and rainforests on both spaces of Orchadia and Earth. We met strange creatures that were so big and some so small we could fit their herd in our palms. Birds and lizards of such colourful variation never seen before by human eyes scattered along us as we ran through each shift.

Little by little, we took apart every shift and reassembled it in such a way to avoid the titanic explosions that had been set position with the shifts to destroy the universe.

'All done!' I said in an extremely tired voice.

'The only thing that is left for us to do is to reduce the double-time reversal symmetry to smithereens, and the universe will be saved, and everything will be in perfect harmony.'

Rasirine and I simultaneously pressed the emitters, and everything blacked out to save the universe.

'Mission accomplished. Let's head back to Orchadia, Ras!'

CHAPTER 37

Rasirine entered the palace and was calling our daughter. 'Lunette! Lunette! Lunette Mum and Dad are back as we have promised you!'

'Mummy, Daddy! You are alive!'

'Well, of course we are back alive, sweetie!' Rasirine responded.

'Where are Grandpa and Grandma, Lunette?' I asked.

Tarnak and Calypso came forward, and they asked us to look at the courtyard, which was filled with hundreds of Neekans bowing down towards us.

Tarnak said, 'You have both accomplished an extraordinary task to neutralise the rapid expansion and contraction of the universe as you were shifting the time lines to bring everything back to normal. Congratulations.'

Tarnak said, 'It is my honour, David, to pass on my crown to you as king of Orchadia. From now on, you will be king an d my daughter will be queen of Orchadia, and together you will lead this planet.'

Tarnak and Calypso crowned us king and queen of Orchadia in the presence of the Neekans who welcomed us with constant clapping and cheering.

'All hail the king and queen of orchadia!' they screamed.

There was a grand ceremony, and the evening ended with an exquisite banquet.

Rasirine and I were tired, so we went to rest. Half way through the night, the strange woman from my childhood dreams reappeared in my mind, but her voice this time was not anxious; it was rather melodious.

The woman then approached me, smiled, and bowed down before she spoke. 'My king of Orchadia, you saved the universe, and you saved Orchadia. You saved the secrets of this planet. You have embedded love for our race despite of your not being a Neekan. Your love for our queen Rasirine is now kept sacred in all the Neekan's hearts. The paradox has been settled.'

The woman left as I watched her dress trail off into mist and fell into a deep slumber with the melody echoing in my ears, which was interrupted by Sofron's voice. 'Next time I will win!'

'Sofron' I responded. 'I believe in this generation of the Neekans, and I believe in my generation and in the next generation of humans, that we will build together a better world and universe!'

Printed in Australia
AUOC02n0940300614
261905AU00003B/3/P